"We agree to have a temporary relationship, right?" Luke said.

"Right. But no strings. No promises." Clem grinned. "No L words."

"And no M words," Luke added with a smile.

"Or even C words," Clem said.

"I *hate* C words," Luke agreed. "I'm committed to too many things as it is."

Clem took a deep breath and extended her right hand.

They solemnly shook hands.

Then, laughing, Luke reached for her. "So what are we waiting for?"

And, seconds later, Clementine Constance Bennelli was in his arms....

Dear Reader,

Spring is just beginning in the month of April for Special Edition!

Award-winning author Laurie Paige presents our THAT'S MY BABY! title for the month, *Molly Darling*. Take one ranching single dad, a proper schoolteacher and an irresistible baby girl, and romance is sure to follow. Don't miss this wonderful story that is sure to melt your heart!

Passions are running high when *New York Times* bestselling author Nora Roberts pits a charming ladies' man against his match—this MacKade brother just doesn't know what hit him in *The Fall of Shane MacKade*, the fourth book in Nora's series, THE MACKADE BROTHERS. Trisha Alexander's new series of weddings and babies, THREE BRIDES AND A BABY, begins this month with *A Bride for Luke*. And Joan Elliott Pickart's THE BABY BET series continues in April with *The Father of Her Child*. Rounding out the month is Jennifer Mikels with the tender *Expecting: Baby*, and Judith Yates's warm family tale, *A Will and a Wedding*.

A whole season of love and romance has just begun from Special Edition! I hope you enjoy each and every story to come!

Sincerely,

Tara Gavin
Senior Editor

Please address questions and book requests to:
Silhouette Reader Service
U.S.: 3010 Walden Ave., P.O. Box 1325, Buffalo, NY 14269
Canadian: P.O. Box 609, Fort Erie, Ont. L2A 5X3

TRISHA ALEXANDER

A BRIDE FOR LUKE

SPECIAL EDITION®

Published by Silhouette Books
America's Publisher of Contemporary Romance

This book is dedicated to Marilyn Amann,
Heather MacAllister and Alaina Richardson, who
held my hand the whole way.

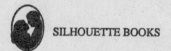 SILHOUETTE BOOKS

ISBN 0-373-24024-4

A BRIDE FOR LUKE

Copyright © 1996 by Patricia A. Kay

This edition published by arrangement with Harlequin Books S.A.

Printed in U.S.A.

TRISHA ALEXANDER

has had a lifelong love affair with books and has always wanted to be a writer. She also loves cats, movies, the ocean, music, Broadway shows, cooking, traveling, being with her family and friends, Cajun food, Calvin and Hobbes and getting mail. Trisha and her husband have three grown children, three adorable grandchildren and live in Houston, Texas. Trisha loves to hear from readers. You can write to her at P.O. Box 441603, Houston, TX 77244-1603.

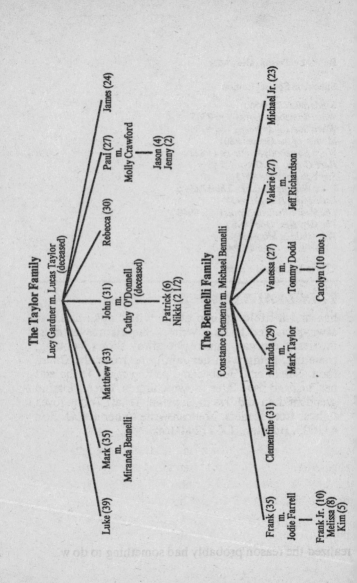

The Taylor Family

Lucy Gardner m. Lucas Taylor
(deceased)

Luke (39) Mark (35) Matthew (33) John (31) Rebecca (30) Paul (27) James (24)
        m.   m.   m.
Miranda Bennelli   Cathy O'Donnell   Molly Crawford
                           (deceased)

Patrick (6)   Jason (4)
Nikki (2 1/2)   Jenny (2)

The Bennelli Family

Constance Clemente m. Michael Bennelli

Frank (35) Clementine (31) Miranda (29) Vanessa (27) Valerie (27) Michael Jr. (23)
   m.   m.   m.   m.
Jodie Farrell   Mark Taylor   Tommy Dodd   Jeff Richardson

Frank Jr. (10)   Carolyn (10 mos.)
Melissa (8)
Kim (5)

Chapter One

"Clem, promise me you'll be on your best behavior today, okay?"

Clementine Constance Bennelli angled an amused look at her younger sister Miranda. "I can't imagine why you think I wouldn't."

Miranda sighed. "C'mon, Clem, don't play games. Just promise."

"Does that mean I have to be sweet and charming? I *hate* being sweet and charming!" To emphasize her point, Clem pressed down on the accelerator and shot through a traffic light that had almost turned red. She bit back a grin as she saw how Miranda grasped the door handle of the Jeep and hung on for dear life.

For some perverse reason, Clem enjoyed scaring the pants off her sisters. In her introspective moments, she realized the reason probably had something to do with their nonstop campaign to reform her and make her into something she had no desire to be—a woman who lived only to please a man.

It constantly amazed Clem that all three of her sisters, who were women of the nineties and should know better, had turned out to be exact replicas of her mother and her aunts—all of whom acted as if attracting and catching a man and then keeping him happy were the most important goals any woman could have.

Clem couldn't understand this attitude. Most of the men she'd met in her thirty-one years weren't half as intelligent or one third as interesting as her women friends.

And men all took themselves so seriously! As if the things they did and the thoughts they thought were of earth-shattering importance.

And, of course, the things Clem did and the thoughts she thought weren't.

This being the case, why on earth would she want to attract and catch one of them? She shuddered at the idea of submerging her goals and desires to some man's.

Of course, men were useful for one thing, she thought with an inward grin.

"Clem?"

Miranda's voice reminded Clem that she'd never actually answered her sister's request. "Okay, okay, I promise not to say or do anything to embarrass you." Then, a few seconds later, feeling momentarily magnanimous, she added, "I know how much it means to you that we make a good impression on the Taylors."

Miranda gave her a grateful smile. "Thanks, Clem. This is awfully important to me. I want Mark's family to like us."

The sisters were on their way to a picnic at Houston's Bear Creek Park. It was the first, but Clem was certain not the last, get-together of the Bennelli and Taylor clans. Miranda had recently become engaged to Mark Taylor, and the Bennellis believed that anyone who married into their family automatically brought his relatives along with him.

Family get-togethers were a ritual, and even Clem—the avowed black sheep and ritual buster—was expected to attend. Most of the time she didn't mind. It wasn't such a big deal, and it pleased her mother.

Besides, being around her sisters always reinforced Clem's ideas about life and what she wanted and didn't want out of hers—not a bad thing, she thought.

"So tell me a little about Mark's family before we get there," Clem said. "That way I won't say anything I shouldn't." For some reason, even when she was trying to be nice, she was always putting her foot in it.

"Well," Miranda responded happily, "he's got five brothers and a sister."

"Guess his parents never heard of birth control, either," Clem said dryly.

"Clem!"

Clem grinned. "Sorry. Go on. What're their names and what're they like?"

"Well, you know Mark's father is dead. He had a heart attack at a pretty young age. I've met his mother—her name is Lucy—and his sister, Rebecca, and his brother Matt. James, the youngest one, is in medical school in Chicago, but I met him New Year's Eve. They're all really nice. I just love his mother. She's a doll. I haven't met Mark's other three brothers, but they should all be there today. There's Paul, who's married, John, whose wife died last year... that was really sad... and Luke, the oldest. At least, I hope Luke is coming today. Mark said Luke mentioned an appointment with a prospective client, so maybe he wouldn't be able to make it."

"Now, wait a minute," Clem said. "Let me see if I've got all this straight. Matthew, Mark, Luke, John, James, Paul and Rebecca?"

"Uh-huh."

Clem laughed. "What happened to Peter and Mary Magdalene?"

"Clem, you *promised!*"

"I'm sorry, I just couldn't help it." She flipped on her right blinker at the approach of Highway 6.

"Mark says Luke is sort of the family rebel ... kind of like you," Miranda said slyly.

"Hmm? Who's a rebel like me?" She was only half listening to Miranda, who tended to ramble.

Clem tapped her horn impatiently. The old geezer in front of her must never have heard that in Texas you can turn right on red.

"Are you listening to me or not?" Miranda asked. "I just told you—Mark's older brother Luke. He's the president of the family's security business where they all work. Luke's sister, Rebecca, told me Luke's a real hunk, and all the women are crazy about him. She said it's almost embarrassing the way they chase after him.

But I guess, like you, he's not interested in getting married.''

"Umm," Clem said. She really didn't care whether he was or not.

"He's going to be Mark's best man, so you'll be paired with him at the wedding. Hey," Miranda added brightly, as if she'd just thought of it, "he's completely unattached, from what Rebecca said. Who knows? Maybe you two'll hit it off."

Not bloody likely, Clem thought. She couldn't stand the type of guy Miranda had described. If women were falling all over them, they usually had a pretty inflated opinion of themselves. But all she said was, "Don't get any ideas."

"I'm not. I just thought—"

"I know what you thought. But I'm not interested in being fixed up. Which I've told you at least a hundred times already."

"I know, I know."

"Then why do you keep trying?"

"Because I think if you met the right guy, you'd change your mind."

"I won't change my mind. Can't you get it through your head? I am perfectly happy the way I am."

"But it's just not *normal* for you to—"

"Miranda!"

"Okay, okay, I'm sorry...." Miranda subsided into silence.

Jeez, Clem thought, why did every blasted female in her family think it was her own personal mission to see that Clem found a man?

As she'd told Miranda, Clem really was perfectly happy the way she was. She ate when and what she wanted to eat. She slept when and where she wanted to sleep. She had great friends to do things with. She had no one except her boss and her Maker to answer to. And that was just the way she liked it.

"Besides," Clem said, "I doubt I'd appeal to Mark's brother. He's probably like all the rest of the guys out there—looking for some nubile young thing who'll hang on his every word and tell him how wonderful he is at least twenty times a day."

Miranda laughed. "When they made you, they left out that gene."

Clem gave her a sideways look. "Why, sugar pie, of course they didn't. I know how to be just as sweet and suffocatin'ly adorin' as the next steel magnolia. I just don't want to," she drawled in an exaggerated accent, batting her eyelashes for effect.

Then she started to laugh, too, and soon the sisters were giggling uncontrollably.

Luke Taylor leaned against a tree trunk and idly watched his mother and sister and sister-in-law as they unpacked picnic baskets and placed the various items of food and utensils on the picnic tables.

He enjoyed watching them. There was something satisfying in the competent way the women moved, their soft laughter and easy camaraderie.

He chewed on a blade of grass and let the warm breeze soothe him. Spring was his favorite time of year, and it was good to be spending a balmy April Saturday afternoon outdoors instead of working, the way he'd worked most Saturdays the past sixteen years. And because it was a rare day off, he'd even brought along his favorite camera and the fifty-millimeter lens he favored. He smiled, thinking that as soon as they finished their meal today, he'd walk around the park and see what kinds of photo opportunities there were.

"Hey, Luke, glad you could make it today."

Luke turned. His brother Mark was walking toward him. Luke smiled. "Yeah, me, too."

Although Luke was curious about Miranda, Mark's fiancée, and it was good to be outdoors on such a nice day, he wasn't particularly excited about meeting her entire family.

But he was going to be Mark's best man, and since their father's death sixteen years earlier, Luke was the acknowledged head of their family, so what real choice had he had but to come today?

He sighed inwardly. More and more often lately he felt smothered by his obligations and responsibilities, yet powerless to do anything to escape them. He wondered if he would ever be free just to think about himself—to do what he wanted to do, when he wanted to do it. He thought longingly of the travel brochures sitting on his desk at home. It was ironic, he thought, that when he'd had the freedom to roam the world and concentrate on his photography, he hadn't had the money, and now that he had the money, he didn't have the freedom. Shaking off the depressing thought, he turned his attention back to his brother.

Mark looked around happily. "I can't wait for you to meet Miranda. You're gonna like her."

Luke nodded. "Mom seems to like her. She's been telling me how perfect she is for you."

Their mother never missed a chance to drop a few hints to Luke about finding a wife of his own. Sometimes she did it slyly, by emphasizing how happy Paul and Mark were or what nice women *they'd* managed to find. She refused to believe that Luke had no desire to marry. She continued to insist he just hadn't met the right woman yet. Luke had given up trying to persuade her otherwise.

"Yeah, they really hit it off." Mark's green eyes shone with pleasure.

Luke thought that if he were the kind of guy who wanted to add yet more responsibility to his life by getting married, he might've been envious of the look of happiness on Mark's face.

"I hear Miranda comes from a big family, too," he said, not because he particularly cared, but because he knew his brother liked to talk about his fiancée.

"Yes. They've almost got as many as we do—there are six kids. She's got three sisters and two brothers. Wait'll you see her two younger sisters. They're twins and they're both knockouts. One of them—Valerie—was Miss Texas four years ago."

"Oh, yeah?" Luke said.

"Yeah, but don't get any ideas. They're both married. The only unattached one in the family is Clem . . . she's a couple of years older than Miranda. She's a reporter for Channel 10."

"Really?" Luke was a Channel 2 man himself.

"Yeah. Ever since Miranda told me about her, I've been watching her. She's pretty good."

Luke didn't feel Mark's statement required an answer, so he didn't give him one.

"Hey, there's Miranda and Clem now!" Mark announced.

Two dark-haired women, one tall, the other shorter and smaller, were walking toward them. The smaller woman waved, and Luke guessed she must be Miranda.

Mark rushed forward, and he and Miranda embraced. The taller woman stood to one side, an indulgent look on her face.

Luke studied her curiously. He estimated her height to be about five feet ten, because she was nearly as tall as Mark. Her getup amused him: baggy khaki shorts with lots of pockets, a white T-shirt with something written in red across the front, brown hiking boots topped by red socks, and a red cap jammed down over gleaming dark hair that hung in one long braid ending just below her shoulder blades.

Nice legs, he thought, giving them an appreciative sweep. Very nice legs. Tanned and shapely and long. Just the way he liked them.

Just then, she looked his way, catching him ogling her legs. He looked up. Dark eyes met his gaze squarely, almost challengingly.

Then, slowly and deliberately, she dropped her gaze to his legs, giving him an identical once-over.

Luke grinned. *Touché.* If he'd had a hat on, he would have tipped it.

An answering amusement sparked her eyes.

Mark, holding Miranda's hand, brought his intended closer. "Honey, this is Luke. Luke, this is Miranda." Pride rang from his voice.

"Hi, Luke. I've heard a lot about you," Miranda said.

"And I've heard a lot about you." He took her free hand and clasped it warmly. "Mark talks of little else." Miranda had a sweet smile, a sweet face, he thought. Her dark blue eyes sparkled with happiness as she looked at Luke, then adoringly up at Mark.

"And this is Clem, Miranda's sister," Mark went on, tearing his gaze away from Miranda and inclining his head toward the tall woman with the amused eyes.

Luke turned slowly. "Hello, Clem."

"Hi." She extended her right hand, giving him a firm handshake. Her hand felt warm and strong and perfectly fitted to his. He was oddly reluctant to release it.

Their gazes held for a long moment. Her eyes were a very dark blue, almost indigo, and fringed by thick black lashes. There was an appealing sprinkle of freckles across her nose, and she wore no makeup except a trace of lipstick on her generous mouth. Of course, she didn't need makeup, he decided. Not when she looked this good without it.

She didn't fidget or look away, and she knew he was studying her. He could see the knowledge of it in her expression. She seemed completely relaxed, as if she didn't give a damn what he was thinking.

That fact alone was enough to intrigue Luke. Most of the women he met tried to impress him. It was refreshing to meet one who didn't.

"Well, come on, honey, I want to introduce you to the rest of the family," Mark said to Miranda.

Miranda looked at her sister. "You want to come, too, Clem?"

"You go on," Clem replied easily. "I'll catch up with you later." As the two lovebirds walked off, Clem turned back to Luke. "Are we the first ones of the Bennelli family to arrive?"

"I think so." He looked down at her T-shirt. It read, Of Course God Created Man First. He Needed A Prototype. Luke grinned again as he met her unwavering gaze.

"Were you reading the motto on my T-shirt or were you staring at my breasts?" she asked.

The grin became a chuckle. "Is there a right answer to that question?"

Now that she'd called his attention to them, he decided her breasts were nice, too—not big, but rounded and well-defined in the snug-fitting shirt.

"You bet there's a right answer," she retorted.

"Let me guess.... The right answer is that I was reading the motto."

"And?"

"And what?"

"And, based on the motto, you think I'm one of those pain-in-the-butt women, the kind you can't stand, right?"

He had a feeling she was a pain in the butt, all right, but she was damned cute. He also had a feeling he'd better not say so. Somehow Luke knew Clem Bennelli would not appreciate being described as cute.

"Are you a mind reader, too?" he asked instead.

She frowned. "Too?"

He tried to keep a straight face, but his mouth refused to do anything but quirk up in amusement. "In addition to being a pain in the butt."

She stared at him. He could tell she was fighting a smile. She lost the fight. "I guess I deserved that."

He decided that a man could lose himself in those eyes of hers. He also decided she had a mouth meant to be kissed. "Is that an apology?"

"I never apologize."

"Why is it I'd already figured that out?"

She shoved her hands into the side pockets of her shorts. The smile faded, and the look she gave him was assessing. "Miranda tells me you're the family rebel. Why is that?"

Luke shrugged. "I guess because I'm different from my brothers."

"I'm different, too," she said proudly. Then, eyes narrowed thoughtfully, she added, "How are you different?"

"Well, I'm pretty much of a loner."

"I'm a loner, myself."

"Yet here we both are..." he said.

"Surrounded by family..." she added.

He smiled down at her.

She smiled up at him.

As their gazes connected, something flared in her eyes, and she slowly licked her lips.

Luke stared at her mouth as desire pierced his gut with surprising intensity. "So why were you and Miranda discussing me?"

Her look turned crafty. "Don't get any ideas."

Luke was getting a lot of ideas, but none that he thought it would be wise to voice. "I wouldn't dream of it."

"She was just briefing me on Mark's family," Clem continued, grinning. "She's always worried I'm going to say something to embarrass her."

"Does she have reason to worry?"

She shrugged. "Maybe. I do have a tendency to say what I think."

"I'd already figured that out."

"The thing is, I think it's stupid to play games. If someone doesn't agree with me, I'd rather have them say so, flat out. But some people get so upset when their opinions are questioned."

"Tough, aren't you?"

"In my business I have to be tough."

Luke would have liked to explore the topic of her business, but just then half a dozen people approached the picnic area, and Clem looked around.

"Oh, there's some of my family. I guess I'd better go join them." She gave him a little salute. "Nice talking to you, Luke."

Luke nodded, watching as she walked away. She had a nice, easy stride—unconsciously provocative in its unstudied grace. As she approached her family, various people turned and greeted her. Soon she was absorbed into the group and she didn't look his way again, but Luke continued to watch her laugh and talk and wave her hands around in animated gestures. Gradually she and her family gravitated toward the covered pavilion, where he could see they were being introduced to his family.

Luke continued to observe them from a distance, his gaze returning to Clem again and again.

Clem Bennelli was a study in contrasts, he decided. Outspoken, obviously opinionated and sexy as hell.

He wasn't even sure if he liked her, but she was the first woman to snag his attention in a long time. He couldn't remember the last time he'd felt that sizzling awareness of a woman during a first meeting.

Warning signals flashed in his head. To act on that awareness might be unwise. Foolhardy, even.

After all, she was Miranda Bennelli's sister and would soon be his brother's sister-in-law. It would be awkward for the entire family if Luke were to become involved with Clem, because it was inevitable that any involvement would eventually come to an end.

Luke was not interested in any kind of permanent commitment, so no other outcome was possible. And in his experience, male-female relationships rarely ended without rancor.

Yes, it would definitely be smart to steer clear of her.

She sure was entertaining, though. And he had a long afternoon to kill. What harm could there be in engaging in some more flirting or verbal sparring with her?

Idly he strolled toward the group.

Chapter Two

Clem decided Luke Taylor was exactly the kind of man she'd expected him to be based on Miranda's description. You could tell just by looking at him—and talking to him hadn't changed her impression—that he thought he was pretty hot stuff. Of course, he did have a sense of humor, she'd give him that.

Yet no matter how many times she reminded herself that, sense of humor or not, he was definitely the kind of man she normally avoided, she couldn't seem to get him out of her mind. She kept watching him surreptitiously as he was introduced to the other members of her family.

He was definitely a hunk, just as Miranda had said. In fact, if Clem were rating him on a hunk scale of one to ten, which she wasn't, he'd be a ten—no sweat.

She reluctantly admitted she liked everything about the way he looked: his height, which she estimated at six feet plus, his lean body, his dark blond hair worn slicked back and a little long, his rugged face, the glint of danger glowing in his green eyes, and his slow, sexy smile.

Oh, boy, that was definitely a killer smile.

She liked the way he was dressed, too—the army green shorts, the worn sneakers and the faded black T-shirt. No-nonsense clothes. Clem hated men who spent more time and money on their wardrobes than she did.

Despite the offhand attire, it didn't surprise her that women were supposedly crazy about him. Good thing she wasn't like most women. Shoot, she could appreciate his sex appeal objectively, no harm in that.

After all, she was a reporter. Just because she'd made the observation that he was attractive didn't mean she was going to fall prey to his charms. Heck, no. She was immune to all that garbage.

Clem knew exactly what she wanted out of life, and kowtowing to a man wasn't it. A man on the scene would just get in the way of her attaining her goals—complicate her life unnecessarily.

Even as she told herself all of this, she slid another glance his way, and just as she did, he looked in her direction.

Clem hurriedly dropped her gaze.

Damn!

Just what she needed—his thinking she was interested in him, or something—which he was sure to think since he'd caught her looking at him. Men always thought you were interested in them when you looked at them.

After all, the majority had egos the size of Texas, so why wouldn't they think so? It would never cross their minds that maybe you felt about them the same way you might feel about a snake—repulsed yet fascinated.

She snuck another peek at him through her lashes. He was still looking at her, and this time he gave her a slow, knowing smile. Her heart increased its tempo as, flustered, she pretended to be absorbed in her plate of barbecue. She hurriedly took a bite, then drank some iced tea, all the while knowing his eyes were still trained her way.

Why did he keep looking at her as if he knew exactly what she was thinking? And why had she ended up at the same table as him when there were three other tables in the pavilion?

"So, it's Clem, isn't it?" said a friendly female voice from across the table.

Clem looked up to meet the warm brown eyes of Luke's brother Paul's wife, who was seated directly across from her. "Yes," she answered, smiling.

"I've watched you on Channel 10," the woman said. "You're great."

"Thanks." Clem tried to remember what the wife's name was. Holly? Molly? Dolly? Why was she so bad at remembering names?

"I loved that piece you did on Sally Martino. 'The Woman Behind the Man.'"

Clem nodded glumly. Her claim to fame. A puff piece. That's all she ever seemed to do. She was dying to cover real news, but Raymond, her boss, kept assigning her to interviews and warm-fuzzy stories. What she wouldn't give for a shot at something important, something that might make the network wire.

"Did you get to meet Chris Martino?" Paul's wife continued eagerly, eyes bright as new pennies.

"He wasn't there during that particular interview," Clem said. "But I've met him before."

"Really? He's so *cute,* don't you think? You're so lucky. I'd *love* to meet him."

Clem resisted the urge to roll her eyes. Is that all Holly-Dolly-Molly could think about? How cute the Rockets' assistant coach was? Personally, Clem would rather meet somebody like that guy from Galveston who was organizing a tax revolt or the policewoman accusing her supervisor of harassment. "Actually, I thought he was kind of stuck on himself," she said.

"Really? Is that what you thought, Luke?" Paul's wife asked. "Luke knows Chris Martino, too," she explained to Clem.

Clem slowly turned her gaze in Luke's direction.

"I wouldn't say I knew him, Molly. The company handled some security for the Rockets last year and I talked with Martino briefly." He met Clem's gaze. "He seemed like a nice enough guy, though."

Clem bristled. She was sure Martino had seemed like a nice enough guy to Luke. After all, Luke was a man. And all men stuck together.

"Oh, Luke's so *modest,*" Molly gushed, batting her big eyes at him. "He knows all *sorts* of famous people. And it's not just because of the business, either.

Why, Baron Luchinski invited Luke to dinner last week.''

Baron Luchinski and his wife were one of the wealthiest couples in Houston and made the local gossip column on a daily basis.

Valerie, one of Clem's sisters, who was sitting at the other end of the table, piped up. "What's the baron like, Luke? Is his home as beautiful as everyone says?"

"You got to see his *home?*" squealed Vanessa, Valerie's twin. "I've heard it's spectacular. Did you know that Madonna once stayed there?"

"Sorry. I didn't pay that much attention to the decor," Luke said. "Besides, Molly's exaggerating. I wasn't really a dinner guest. I was providing undercover security."

Valerie's eyes widened. "Were you there the night Sean Connery was there?"

Luke nodded. "Yeah, that was the night."

"Oh, my gosh, I read all about that dinner party in Maxine's column," Valerie said. "Is Sean Connery as gorgeous in person as he is in the movies?"

Luke smiled. "Afraid I didn't notice." The smile got wider. "He's not my type."

Valerie giggled. "I didn't think he was," she returned coyly.

Oh, barf, Clem thought. What was wrong with these women? Couldn't they think of anything more important to talk about? "What do you all think about the president's decision to send troops to San Carlos?" she asked as soon as there was a lull in the conversation. If she had to sit here, she refused to be bored silly.

"Oh, Clem, let's not talk about depressing stuff. Not today," Miranda said.

"I agree," Vanessa added fervently. "Tell us more about your work, Luke. What other famous people have you met?"

But Luke didn't answer Vanessa. Instead, he turned his eyes Clem's way and said, "I don't think the president had a choice."

Clem would have liked to disagree with him, just on general principles, but she couldn't because she didn't think the president had had a choice, either.

"I do think the network's coverage has been great," Vanessa said. She grinned. "That Drew McLaine is really something, isn't he? So-o-o sexy."

If there was anything Clem hated, it was mention of Drew McLaine, the network golden boy, who had the kind of job and the kinds of assignments Clem coveted most in the world. "If I could ever get a shot at a story like that, I'd show him a thing or two," she grumbled.

"I, for one, am glad the station *doesn't* give you dangerous assignments," Miranda interjected. "Mom and Dad would have a conniption fit worrying about you."

"Is that the kind of story you want to be reporting?" Luke asked.

Clem immediately felt defensive, even though his tone was mild. "Yes, it is."

He nodded thoughtfully.

She waited for him to say something else, and when he didn't, she said, "I suppose you think women aren't capable of reporting anything serious, like a war."

"Oh, Clem." Miranda sighed. "Not that subject again."

"I'm sure there are hundreds of women perfectly capable of reporting wars or anything else. But—" Luke stopped.

"But what?" Clem said.

"Well . . . it's not safe in places like San Carlos."

"So? It's not safe for the soldiers or Drew Mc-Laine, either."

"But they're men," Luke noted.

"Hear, hear," Mark said from the end of the table.

"I suppose you think a woman's place is in the kitchen." Clem stared him straight in the eye. "Or in the bedroom."

She could see he was fighting a smile. Oh, that infuriated her! There was nothing Clem hated more than a man who didn't take her seriously.

"You're putting words in my mouth," he protested.

"Oh, come on, admit it," Clem fired back. "That's *exactly* what you believe. That's what *all* men believe. God! I'm so sick of that attitude! I have to contend with that attitude every day."

Miranda's voice was plaintive. "Could we please change the subject?"

"I'm still waiting to hear what other famous people Luke has guarded," Valerie said. "I just think your business is fascinatin'." She gave Luke one of her brilliant smiles—perfected in the dozens of beauty contests she'd participated in since her teen years.

Clem scowled and decided she couldn't sit there one more minute and listen to her sisters gush all over Luke. She looked around and saw that some of the others had finished eating and were organizing a softball game. "I think I'll go join the softball game," she said, rising. She picked up her plastic plate and utensils and headed for the trash barrel.

She decided it was probably her fairy godmother looking out for her when she'd ended up at the same lunch table as Luke. If she hadn't seen for herself that he was exactly the kind of man she wouldn't touch with a ten foot pole, she might have been tempted to explore the physical attraction she'd felt between them.

So why, if she knew that, did she feel oddly disappointed?

Luke watched Clem Bennelli stride off, her cute fanny twitching above those long, gorgeous legs, and wondered what she would be like in the sack. Not that he intended to find out, of course.

He wasn't crazy.

But it was fun to wonder.

After he finished his lunch, he picked up his camera equipment and wandered over to the softball field, where he saw Clem's mother sitting on a bench watching the game.

When he reached her, he propped one leg on the bench. "Who's winning?" he asked.

Connie Bennelli turned to look at him, and he noticed that her eyes were the same color as Clem's. She smiled. "We are."

Luke grinned. "Doesn't surprise me. No one in my family is very athletic. We try hard, though."

For a moment he watched the boisterous game. He noticed that Clem was playing second base. His grin expanded as he saw that she'd turned her cap around so that the bill was in the back. She crouched just to the left of the base, her right hand punching her gloved left hand, legs spread apart, rocking back and forth as she alternately watched the batter and the runner on first base.

"Steee-rike three!" yelled the umpire.

Various Bennellis jumped around and clapped each other on the back, including Clem.

Luke's fingers itched, and he hurriedly opened his camera bag and withdrew his equipment. He snapped on the lens, adjusted the aperture and shutter speeds, and looked through the viewfinder. As the game resumed he quickly shot a roll of film, finding himself concentrating on Clem Bennelli more often than not.

"So you're the oldest in the family," Connie Bennelli said as the teams changed sides and Luke lowered his camera.

"Yes."

"And the president of the family business . . ."

Luke smiled. "Yeah, I became president by default."

Connie nodded, and Luke figured she knew about his father's death and why Luke had ended up running the company.

"Miranda tells me it's a very successful business."

"Yes, we've been lucky. Things have worked out well." It was his standard answer. But it wasn't the whole truth. Things had worked out well in that he had been able to find a way to keep his family afloat after his father's untimely death when he was only forty-two and Luke was only twenty-two. But working his butt off sixty and seventy hours a week for sixteen years in a business he'd never had any desire to be part of wasn't Luke's idea of things working out well for him personally.

He had never wanted this kind of responsibility. He had had a completely different idea of what his life would be like. If he had been able to follow his own dream, he would be working all over the world, seeing and photographing all the places and people he'd only read about. He'd be involved in work he loved, free to take any assignment. He'd have no shackles. No one to take care of. No one to worry about. And only himself to answer to.

Connie started to say something else, then her attention was diverted as her husband came up to bat.

Luke shook off his thoughts and turned his attention back to the game, watching the remainder while resisting all efforts by his family to get him to come and play. The game ended with Clem hitting a bases-loaded home run, and Luke captured her triumphant slide into home plate in a series of pictures taken using the power winder so he wouldn't miss any of the fast action. When he finally lowered his camera, he was sure he'd gotten some great shots.

Connie smiled at Luke. "That equipment looks pretty serious. You must be a real photography buff."

Luke nodded. "Yeah, I've always loved it."

"When I take pictures, I usually manage to chop off the people's heads."

Luke laughed. "So does my mother."

"Well . . . it's been nice talking to you." Connie got up, smiled goodbye, then wandered off toward the pavilion.

Luke waited. After a while, Clem ambled over his way.

"Good game," he said. "That was a great hit you had."

She grinned, obviously delighted with herself. Drops of moisture beaded her forehead and nose, her face was flushed and those magnificent eyes of hers sparkled. Her cap was still turned backward, and her T-shirt clung damply to her chest. Luke thought she looked even more sexy and appealing than she had before.

"Yeah, it was, wasn't it? So why didn't you join us?"

He shrugged. "I'm not crazy about sports. Besides, I was photographing the action." He pointed to his camera bag.

She nodded. "I saw you. But I thought all men loved games." Now her smile changed from self-satisfied to amused.

"Some games." At that moment, looking at her, breathing in her musky scent, Luke was seized by the urge to yank her into his arms and plant a kiss right in the middle of her sexy mouth.

Their gazes clung, awareness sizzling in the air between them. Her smile slowly faded. Luke knew that she knew exactly what he was thinking.

After a long moment she gave herself a little shake, then said, avoiding his gaze, "I'm thirsty. I think I'll go get something to drink."

He didn't answer.

Somehow it seemed safer that way.

* * *

Whew, Clem thought as she walked away, the look in Luke Taylor's eyes was hot enough to ignite a forest fire, which was exactly what it had done to her innards. She couldn't remember the last time she'd felt so dangerously attracted to a man, so completely aware of him sexually.

She walked over to the pavilion and helped herself to some iced tea from the big urn sitting at the end of one of the tables. Using napkins to blot her sweaty face, she stood there and thought about whether it might not be wise to heed all those danger signals going off in her brain and get the hell out of Dodge.

And speaking of the cause of those danger signals, there he was. She watched covertly as Luke walked up to a little knot of men consisting of his brothers Mark and Matthew, Clem's father, Mike, and Valerie's husband, Jeff. They widened their circle to include Luke, and the five of them stood talking for a while.

Clem couldn't help but notice how favorably Luke compared to the others. He was the tallest of the group and by far the sexiest and most attractive. She could easily understand why women chased him, as Miranda had disclosed earlier. Men like Luke didn't grow on trees.

Yeah, well, men like Luke do not fit into your agenda, either, remember that. Men like Luke are trouble. Men like Luke throw monkey wrenches into carefully laid out life plans.

Clem sighed and finished off her tea in a large gulp, then walked purposefully over to the group of men and said, ''Well, I've gotta take off. It's been fun, Mark. I really enjoyed it." Her gaze slowly swung around. "Nice meeting you, Matthew...Luke." Turning to her father, she said, "Bye, Dad. See you tomorrow." Avoiding Luke's gaze, she kissed her father's cheek, waved cheerily and strode off to say her goodbyes to the remainder of the family.

She hated the fact that she was running away. Clem prided herself on the knowledge that she never ran away from anything. She had always faced every challenge head-on.

She told herself there was a first time for everything, and the wise person knew when that time had come.

"And that's *all?*" Annie Stratton, Clem's best friend, exclaimed, her voice filled with disappointment. "You just walked *away?* You didn't even talk to him again?"

"Yes, I walked away. No, I didn't talk to him again," Clem said. "What else did you expect?"

"I don't know.... *Something.* I guess I was hoping he got carried away by this tremendous force between the two of you and followed you to your car where he swept you into his arms, kissed you and said he just *had* to see you again...." Annie's dramatic sigh carried clearly over the telephone wire.

"Oh, pul-*leese!*" Clem was sorry she'd told her friend about Luke Taylor. Annie was an incurable romantic. A naive incurable romantic. "Life isn't a fairy tale, Annie."

"I know, I know...."

"Not everyone is like you and Bradley." Bradley Winthrop Stratton was Annie's husband. Her adoring, prince-on-a-white-horse husband who worshiped the ground Annie walked on. Well, actually, the horse he normally rode was a dappled gray, but the semantics weren't important.

"I know," Annie repeated. "I realize not everyone can be as lucky as I've—"

"Look," Clem interrupted firmly, "I'm glad you're happy. I really am. But I'm happy, too. Believe it or not, every woman does not need, or even want, a man in her life to be happy."

"Well, if you say so," Annie said doubtfully.

Clem knew she wasn't convinced. This wasn't the first time the two of them had had this particular conversation. Annie really thought all it would take for Clem to change her mind about needing and wanting a man was the right man. Well, the right man hadn't been invented who would change Clem's mind on this subject.

And Luke Taylor wasn't even *close!*

"Despite what you say, you must have *some* interest in him," Annie observed. "Otherwise, why have you spent the past fifteen minutes telling me about him?"

"Why is it that you pick the darnedest times to get logical?" Clem retorted, smiling in spite of herself.

"Well? Don't you?"

"Don't I what?"

"Come on, Clem, quit pretending you don't know what I'm talking about."

Clem expelled a noisy sigh. "Oh, all right, you win! Yes, he does interest me."

Annie giggled. "I thought so."

"*Well,*" Clem said defensively, "he's *sexy!* He's the kind of guy you fantasize about making love to. After all, I'm *normal* when it comes to physical needs!"

"I see...."

"But that's all, and I don't intend to do anything about it."

"Oh, Clem, why not?"

"Because the only kind of guy I'm interested in is the kind I can walk away from easily. It's just not smart to mess with any other kind."

"But, Clem, then you'll *never* get married."

"That's the idea, Annie. That's what I've been telling you for years. I *do not want* to get married. I want no permanent commitments of any kind. I can't afford permanent commitments, not if I want to achieve my career goals."

"But what if you change your mind? Then it might be too late."

"I'll never change my mind. I plan on blowing this town just as soon as I get the chance. When my big break comes, I'm outta here. And I don't want anyone or anything standing in my way."

As soon as Luke got home that night he headed straight for his darkroom. He was even more eager than usual to get his pictures developed, because he had a feeling Clem Bennelli was a photographer's dream.

He wasn't disappointed.

As he hung the wet prints up to dry, he could see that his instincts had been right on target. There wasn't a bad picture of Clem in the lot. And two in particular were very good—one of the shots of her sliding into home plate and one where she was jumping gleefully, a expression of pure joy and exhilaration on her face.

He studied the pictures a long time.

They produced an emotion in him that was hard to define. It wasn't desire, although Clem Bennelli was eminently desirable. No, it was more like...envy. Because Clem Bennelli obviously had a passion for life and it showed in everything she did and said. Luke knew Clem was the kind of person who was never bored.

Luke was bored most of the time.

He wanted, more than anything, to feel enthusiastic about life. To look forward to getting up each morning. To have a goal in life that he was actively working toward. And he knew that wasn't going to happen until he could get out from under the weight of his responsibilities. If only he could just say, "The hell with it," and quit. But how could he? The business provided the bulk of his mother's income, and it supported all of his siblings and their families. And every single one of them had resisted his efforts to involve them in the day-to-day management of the company. They all wanted to do their jobs and go home at the end of the day and forget about everything.

But Luke couldn't forget.

Because, after all, someone had to worry. Someone had to do the nitty-gritty work.

Yet as long as he continued to accept responsibility, his brothers and sister would let him. And if he walked away from the company, without anyone knowing anything about running it or bringing in new business, it would go under. Poorly managed companies simply didn't survive in today's competitive marketplace.

Luke closed his eyes, leaning against his worktable. He was in a catch-22 situation.

Damned if he did. Damned if he didn't.

And he didn't see how anything would ever change.

"So what did you think of her?" asked Mark the following day. The entire clan had come to the Taylor house for dinner, and now the women were cleaning up, and Mark and Luke had walked outside to enjoy the sunny day.

"Who?" replied Luke. His gaze swept appreciatively around his mother's yard, taking in the rainbow of colors from the palest pink roses to deep purple verbena to scarlet geraniums.

Mark smiled slyly. "You know who. Miranda's sister. Clem, the reporter. The woman you spent nearly the whole day yesterday talking to."

"Oh. Her."

Mark's smile became a knowing grin. "Don't pretend you're not interested, 'cause I watched you. You were ogling her."

"I don't ogle."

"Call it whatever you want. You couldn't take your eyes off the woman."

Luke gave his brother a hard-eyed glare, but it didn't work. The silly grin on Mark's face remained there.

"Come on, you can tell me," Mark said. "You planning to ask her out?"

Luke shook his head. "Not a chance."

"Why not?"

"For starters, she's too noisy, stubborn and opinionated."

Mark laughed. "Yeah, well, maybe. But she's also *exactly* the kind of woman you're always insisting you want."

"You're crazy."

"Haven't you been telling me for years now that you can't stand the clinging-vine type? The kind that parrots everything you say and has no opinions of her own? That you'd love to meet a woman who's independent and not looking for a man to take care of her?"

"Yes, but—"

"But nothing! That's exactly what you've been saying," Mark said triumphantly.

"Look, Mark, forget it, will you? I am not, n-o-t, *not* interested in her. Now, let's drop the subject."

Later, after Mark and Miranda and most of his other siblings had gone their separate ways, Luke thought about his conversation with his brother. He hoped he had managed to convince Mark that he wasn't interested in Clem Bennelli. It would never do for Mark to realize how close he'd come when he'd said Luke was ogling her.

Luke wondered what Mark would think if he could have seen Luke developing all those pictures of her last night. He'd never hear the end of it.

But it didn't matter that Mark was right—that feisty, opinionated, passionate-about-life Clem was exactly the kind of woman Luke would enjoy getting to know. He couldn't afford to indulge his interest. Now, if she were anyone other than Miranda's sister . . .

But she wasn't.

So no matter what Mark or anyone else had to say about the subject, Luke was not going to pursue any kind of relationship with Clem Bennelli.

Period.

"She's perfect for him," Miranda said. She smiled up at Mark. "Absolutely perfect." It was Sunday evening, and the two of them were sitting on the couch at Miranda's apartment.

"I know." He put his arm around her and nuzzled her cheek. He loved the way she smelled—sweet and fresh, like wildflowers and sunshine. He pressed his nose closer, then dropped his mouth lower to nibble at her neck.

She giggled. "That tickles." She batted him away. "Come on. Let's talk for a while. How are we going to get those two together?"

Mark pulled back. "Wait a minute. *We* are not going to do anything. We've already done our part. We introduced them. Anything else is up to them."

Miranda sighed. "But Mark, I talked to her this morning, and she says she's not interested, and you said he said the same thing when you talked to him this afternoon."

"He did. Emphatically."

"That means they need some help!"

Mark hated it when Miranda looked at him like that. He always ended up giving in to her. He framed his words carefully. "C'mon, sweetheart, be reasonable. Messing around in other people's love lives is just asking for trouble. It'd be bad enough if we were trying to fix up two friends, but Clem's your sister, and Luke's my brother.''

"I know," Miranda said, her pouty mouth getting poutier by the minute. "That's why it's so *important* to do this exactly right."

"That's why it's so important to forget it!"

"Mark..."

He moaned. "Miranda, honey, please. I'm telling you, Luke'll be royally ticked if we try anything cute, and I don't like being on the receiving end when he loses his temper."

"They don't have to *know* what we're doing," Miranda persisted obstinately, her chin set at that angle Mark knew so well.

Now it was Mark's turn to sigh. This was a losing battle. He might as well stop struggling. "What do you want to do?" he asked resignedly.

Miranda grinned. "Well, I was thinking..."

Chapter Three

Luke enjoyed cooking, and Monday night—home early by design—he felt like eating Chinese, so he took a frozen chicken breast out of the freezer and put it in the microwave to defrost. Then he sliced some fresh mushrooms and green onions and broccoli, added some snow peas and dumped them into his wok with a little peanut oil.

He debated between making rice or using crispy noodles for his stir fry. While trying to decide which he preferred, he switched on the small TV set that sat on one end of the bar dividing his kitchen from his eating area. The Channel 2 six-o'clock news was just starting, with Bill Balleza introducing the lead story.

On a sudden whim, Luke changed the channel to 10. He told himself it was just idle curiosity prompting him to see if Clem showed up on the newscast.

The microwave pinged, so he removed the chicken, sliced it and added it to the ingredients in the wok. He stirred for a while, then, having decided he wanted rice, he measured out the correct amounts of water and rice and put it on to cook, as well.

Next he seasoned his vegetables and chicken with Chinese spices and a little white wine and soy sauce, all the while keeping one eye and ear tuned to the newscast.

Clem Bennelli didn't appear, and Luke was half amused, half irritated to find he was disappointed.

For the rest of the evening, as Luke ate his dinner and cleaned up the kitchen, he continued to think about Clem. He took his coffee and some paperwork out to his tiled patio, where the spring breeze had set his wind chimes to a merry tinkling and the fountain in the center of the walled area provided a soothing gurgle.

It was irritating how he couldn't seem to get her out of his mind. As much as he had been telling himself there was no room in his life for anyone, much less Mark's future sister-in-law, he couldn't help remembering how much fun it had been to spar with her at the picnic.

He grinned.

She was one of the most interesting and intriguing females he'd ever set eyes on. A real study in contrasts with that tough, don't-mess-with-me exterior disguising what Luke was sure was a warm, completely feminine woman underneath.

It was really too bad. It would probably be a lot of fun—not to mention a real challenge—to plumb those inner depths.

And why was he still thinking about the possibility? Hadn't he already decided Clem Bennelli was off-limits? Hadn't he told his brother so, in no uncertain terms?

Forget it, he told himself, turning to the unread report on his lap. Just forget it.

Clem felt too itchy to sit around her apartment Monday night. Truth be told, she didn't like her efficiency apartment much. It was just a place to hang her hat. She slept on a futon, ate on a card table and watched a rented TV from a beanbag chair. She hadn't bothered furnishing or decorating it because she didn't plan to be there long. Only until her big break. And then, as she'd reminded Annie the day before, she was out of there.

She'd had a god-awful day. She was working on a story about discipline problems at the high school level, and she'd spent the day editing down the reams of footage in the can, trying to get something dramatic and worthwhile out of the mess.

She hated this kind of soft-core news, which really wasn't news at all, in her opinion. If only she could get Raymond, her boss, to assign her to the kinds of stories he gave Charles Frey and Jack Flannigan, two male co-workers.

Dream on, Bennelli.

Restless and bored, frustrated by the lack of forward motion in her career and her life goals, she decided to go out for a burger at the neighborhood ice house. Maybe some of the locals would be there, and she could drum up a game of pool. She grabbed her shoulder bag and was hunting for her car keys when the phone rang. She debated ignoring it, but she had this thing about telephone calls. Who knew? It might be something important. Maybe a war had broken out, and Raymond had decided to send her into action.

She grinned at her foolishness and walked over to the phone. "Hello?"

"Clem?"

"Oh. Hi, Miranda."

"Well, try to contain your joy," her sister said dryly.

"Sorry. What's up?"

"Nothing. I just wanted to talk. See how you were doing."

Clem frowned. "I'm fine." What did Miranda want? She rarely called just to chitchat. She knew Clem wasn't the chitchatty type.

"Well, I have to admit it . . . I was kind of curious," Miranda said slowly.

"About what?"

"Well . . . did Luke by any chance call you?"

"Luke? Why would *he* call me?"

"Well, I promised Mark I wouldn't say anything, but you won't tell anyone, will you?"

"Tell anyone *what?* Quit talking in riddles, Miranda."

Miranda giggled, then lowered her voice conspiratorially. "This is really funny, but Mark told me, in the strictest confidence, of course, that his brother Luke has got the *biggest* crush on you."

The strangest sensation skidded through Clem, making it a little hard to breathe. "Oh, come on, Miranda," she finally said. "That's hard to believe. I thought you said women fall all over him."

"They do! That's why this is so funny. That he should pick you, and you're not even interested! It's really a hoot, don't you think?"

Clem swallowed. "Yeah, a hoot." She cleared her throat. "Are you sure you're not making this up?"

"Making this *up!*" Miranda squealed. "Oh, come on, Clem, didn't you notice how he kept looking at you on Saturday?"

Well, yeah, Clem had noticed. Plus, she was just about certain he'd been taking pictures of *her* during the softball game. "Why are you telling me this now?" she asked suspiciously.

"Because I thought you'd get a kick out of it."

Clem wouldn't have admitted it if Miranda had held a gun to her head, but she was getting a kick out of it. In fact, for the rest of the evening she thought of little else. It even drove her job frustrations out of her mind.

But something puzzled her. Why on earth had Luke Taylor told his brother something like that? It was the kind of confidence women exchanged, not men. Now, she might have believed it if Luke had said something about the sexual sizzle between them, but a *crush* on her?

Then she smiled.

He probably *had* said something more along the lines of the physical attraction she'd sensed. Mark had probably just prettied it up for Miranda, since Miranda was such a ninny about that kind of stuff.

That must be it.

Clem grinned. Shoot, she'd been thinking the same things about Luke. Well, thinking didn't hurt a thing, as long as the thoughts weren't turned into actions.

And they wouldn't be.

So she was safe.

At ten-thirty, after watching the late news on Channel 10 again, Luke poured himself a snifter of brandy and headed for the Jacuzzi. He sighed with pleasure as he lowered himself into the hot, soapy water. Two seconds later the phone rang.

Moaning inwardly, he picked up the portable phone from the little wicker table sitting next to the Jacuzzi and said resignedly, "Hello."

"Hey, Luke, it's Mark."

"Yeah?"

"You busy?"

"Kind of. I just got in the Jacuzzi."

"Oh, sorry, I won't keep you long. I just, uh, wanted to tell you something I thought you'd get a charge out of."

"What's that?" Luke reached for the snifter of brandy.

"Don't say anything to anyone else about this, okay?"

"Okay." Luke sipped at the brandy.

Mark chuckled. "Well, this is really kinda funny, considering what you think of her, but Miranda told me that Clem told her she's got a really big crush on you and was hoping you were gonna ask her out."

Luke choked and nearly dropped the brandy glass into the water.

"Luke? You okay?"

"Uh, yeah, I'm fine," Luke sputtered. "I just choked on my brandy, that's all."

"Isn't that funny?"

Luke couldn't believe it. Clem Bennelli simply didn't strike him as the type to tell anyone, even her sister, that she had a crush on a guy. Yet it was undeniable that there had been a powerful attraction between them. "Uh, yeah," he answered after a moment, "that's pretty funny."

"I thought you'd appreciate it," Mark said. "Well, I won't keep you. Just wanted to pass that on. Enjoy your Jacuzzi."

Luke could have sworn he heard a faint giggle in the background just as Mark hung up the phone.

"Do you think it worked?" asked Miranda.

"I'm not sure," Mark said.

"Well, what did he say?"

"Not a whole hell of a lot."

"Oh."

She looked and sounded so disappointed, Mark relented. "But he choked on his brandy."

"Does that mean something?"

Mark grinned slowly. "I think it means he swallowed more than the liquor."

After a moment Miranda grinned, too. "Saturday night ought to be interesting, then. Because I'm positive Clem went for it, too."

For the rest of the week Clem found herself unable to stop thinking about Luke Taylor. Feeling really ridiculous, just like a silly teenager, she even found herself driving past his place of business.

Next thing she'd be calling his home and hanging up when he answered, she thought with a grin.

She even wondered if Raymond would be interested in an in-depth look at the personal security business in Houston, then chided herself for trying to find an excuse to see Luke Taylor again.

Besides, she really didn't need to find an excuse, did she, as Miranda had reminded her only this morning. Because Annie was hosting a couples shower for Mark and Miranda Saturday night, and Luke, as the best man, would be there.

And then, of course, there was the rehearsal dinner and the wedding. So she'd see him not just once, but several more times.

She smiled.

If nothing else, at least the next weeks would be interesting.

All week Luke had fought to keep thoughts of Clem out of his mind. Yet each evening, despite his best efforts, he found himself tuning in to the Channel 10 news. And each night, as he sat on his patio, visions of her big eyes and her sexy smile insinuated themselves in his head.

It was the first time in his life that thoughts of a woman had so obsessed him, and he found the situation unnerving.

On Friday afternoon, though, the only thoughts occupying Luke's mind had to do with the business. He was sitting at his desk, working on the May schedule, when Mark walked in. "Hey, Luke, do you want a ride tomorrow night? Miranda and I'll be glad to pick you up."

Luke frowned. "A ride? To where?"

"The couples shower. You know, the one being given out at the Stratton Ranch. I told you about it."

Luke rubbed his eyes. "Sorry. I guess I forgot."

"How could you have forgotten?"

Luke shrugged. "I don't know. We've been so damned busy, it just slipped my mind." He grimaced at his computer screen. "All of this paperwork and planning and scheduling and reporting is enough to drive me crazy. I'm going to be here until at least ten o'clock tonight, and I'll probably have to work all day tomorrow."

"Man, I'm glad I don't have to mess with that stuff," Mark said. "I'd *never* want your job."

Luke felt like saying *he* didn't want his job, either, but *he* hadn't been given a choice. But he didn't for two reasons. The first was this situation wasn't Mark's fault, so why should Luke try to make him feel guilty? And the second was Luke wasn't a whiner. It was one thing to feel sorry for yourself in private. It was quite another to do it out loud. No, until he figured a way out of his dilemma, he'd keep his mouth shut.

"Now what about tomorrow night?" Mark continued, oblivious to Luke's inner turmoil. "Do you want us to pick you up?"

Luke shook his head. "No, that's all right. I'll drive myself." At least that way he'd be free to leave whenever he wanted. "Do I need to do anything? Bring anything?"

"No. Just be there."

"Where is this ranch located again?"

After Mark left his office, Luke turned back to his computer screen and the May schedule, but his concentration was shot. So he would see Clem Bennelli again on Saturday night.

He smiled.

If nothing else, the evening should be interesting.

Saturday turned out to be a glorious spring day with a cornflower blue sky, the silkiest of breezes and no humidity. Clem had to work Saturday morning wrapping up the piece on schools, but Saturday afternoon, after looking at every single piece of clothing in her closet and dismissing them all, she decided she needed a new dress for the party that evening. So she drove to Alaina's, her favorite boutique in the Village.

The owner, a fellow Rice graduate who had given up her geology career in the oil crunch of the early eighties, was an attractive woman with spiked hair and a great sense of style. She'd helped Clem before when Clem needed something special.

"I want something knock-your-eyes-out sexy," Clem said, grinning.

"Hmm," Alaina responded. She walked over to an alcove of dresses, riffled through them and selected a few. "This is my favorite." She held up a black crepe slip dress. "It's perfect for you."

Clem tried them all on, but just as Alaina had said, Clem loved the black dress best. It felt wonderful and it was definitely sexy. She bought it, along with a black strapless bra and sheer black stockings. She decided the black high-heeled sandals she'd bought in a fit of madness two Christmases ago would go perfectly with the new outfit. She smiled happily as Alaina rang up her purchases.

"What about earrings?" Alaina said.

"I don't wear earrings. They hurt my ears."

"Didn't your mother ever tell you about suffering to be beautiful?"

"Only about six million times."

Alaina laughed. "Well, grin and bear it, because this dress cries out for earrings." She reached into the glass-topped case where the costume jewelry was displayed and removed rhinestone waterfalls.

Clem knew she'd truly lost her mind when the earrings joined her other purchases.

But Alaina had been right, Clem thought as she clipped on the earrings a few hours later and looked at herself in the mirror. They really did add just the right touch to her outfit. Clem twisted this way and that, trying to view herself from all angles. She didn't wear all this fancy stuff very often, and she felt a little weird, like a kid playing dress-up.

You don't look anything like a kid.

No, she thought, deciding to go the whole route. She reached for the bottle of perfume her sister Valerie had given her for Christmas. She didn't look the least bit like a kid. She looked like a grown woman.

A woman who is trying to snare a man.

"Oh, shut up," Clem muttered aloud. "It's no big deal if I want to look sexy for a change. It doesn't mean a thing!"

But even as she said it, she knew she was lying to herself. Maybe she wasn't trying to snare Luke, exactly. But she sure did want to knock his eyes out.

Luke's eyes nearly popped out of his head when Clem walked in the door of the Stratton house. He'd thought she looked sexy last weekend at the picnic, but her appearance there was nunlike compared to the way she looked tonight.

Every male hormone in his body stirred to active life as she strolled into the room along with one of her twin sisters—Vanessa, he thought—and Vanessa's husband. He could hardly breathe as he watched Clem greeting the other guests.

She looked . . . incredible.

He couldn't take his eyes off her. Her short black dress undulated over her firm, lightly muscled torso, curving lovingly around her breasts, hips and delectable rump.

And those legs!

Luke wasn't sure his heart could take looking at her legs. Her legs were nothing short of spectacular. He wet suddenly dry lips as images of long, gorgeous legs twined around him pulsated in his mind.

My God, man, get a grip on yourself.

"Wow, Clem, you look great!" said the other twin.

"Thanks. You do, too." Clem smiled at her sister, then let her gaze wander slowly around the room.

It stopped when it reached Luke.

The smile faded.

Their gazes locked.

"I thought you said you didn't ogle," Mark said sotto voce.

Luke jumped.

Clem blinked and looked away.

"I'm going to kill you," Luke growled between gritted teeth. "Don't sneak up on me like that."

Mark smiled slyly. "She's pretty hot stuff, isn't she? This is the first time I've seen her looking like a girl."

In Luke's opinion, Clem didn't look like a girl at all. She looked like a fully grown, sexy, eminently desirable woman, but he thought it wiser not to say so.

Mark chuckled and walked away.

Luke headed for the bar.

Clem licked her lips.

If she had thought Luke looked good on the previous Saturday, that was nothing compared to the way he looked tonight. Tonight he looked as if he'd stepped right out of the pages of *Gentleman's Quarterly,* irresistibly sexy and gorgeous in a pale gray Armani suit and charcoal collarless shirt. All Clem's ideas about men who took such care with their appearance—men who looked better than she did, men who were obviously studs—faded from her mind.

Oh, wow, she thought. Resisting him was going to be no easy task. She was so wrapped up in her thoughts she didn't realize Annie had walked up to her until she spoke.

"Clem, you look beautiful tonight," Annie said, hugging her. Then she lowered her voice to a confidential whisper. "You were right about Luke Taylor. He's *gorgeous!*"

"And speaking of gorgeous, you don't look so bad yourself," Clem returned in an effort to distract Annie from the subject of Luke. Of course, Annie *did* look gorgeous, but then, she always did. Tonight her long, thick, curly, strawberry blond hair and dreamy blue eyes were perfectly showcased in a pale blue satin palazzo-pants outfit, offset by the magnificent double rope of pearls that had been a wedding gift from Bradley. "By the way, where is Bradley? I haven't seen him yet."

"Supervising the preparation of the paella. You know how particular he is." Annie's smile was indulgent.

Clem grinned. Bradley Stratton was the most unlikely gourmet chef you'd ever want to meet. Big, bluff and hearty, he looked as if he lived on steak and potatoes. Instead, he had a sophisticated palate and knew more about cooking than Annie and Clem and all their friends put together.

"Think I'll go say hi to him," Clem said.

She was waylaid several times on her way to the kitchen—the last time by Miranda, who gave her a mischievous grin and said, "My, my, just who are we trying to impress tonight?"

"Whom," Clem corrected automatically. "And I'm not trying to impress anyone. You told me yourself it would be a dress-up night."

Miranda chuckled. "Yes, but I only meant to stop you from showing up in combat boots and army fatigues."

Clem smiled sheepishly. In her younger days she'd been inclined to do just that in an immature nose-thumbing toward convention.

"Anyway, dear sister," Miranda continued, "you look terrific."

"Thanks."

Miranda leaned closer. "Have you talked to Luke yet?"

"Not yet," Clem replied as casually as she could manage. "You know, Miranda, the more I think about it, the more I think Mark must have exaggerated about...you know...Luke's supposed interest in me."

"Oh, no," Miranda assured her fervently, "he didn't. In fact, on the way here tonight he said Luke has been talking about you all week."

"Why hasn't he made some kind of move, then?"

"Well, he thinks you're not interested in *him*. And you know how men are. Their egos can't take much rejection."

Clem frowned. Luke struck her as the kind of man who would naturally assume *every* woman would be interested in him. She opened her mouth to say so.

"Oh, here he comes now," Miranda hurriedly murmured. She looked up and smiled brightly.

A few seconds later, from behind Clem, Luke's voice said, "You two look as if you're discussing something of earthshaking importance."

Clem turned slowly. She told herself to be cool, but the moment her eyes met his, her stupid heart picked up its pace. God, she hated that! Why *couldn't* she control her body? "Actually," she drawled, "we were talking about you, so it wasn't important at all."

He grinned.

"Oh, Clem's just kidding," Miranda said, her eyes saying, *Clem, how could you?*

"I don't think Clem kids," Luke replied. "I think she says exactly what she means."

"To the extreme discomfort of my family," Clem observed.

Luke laughed.

Miranda cleared her throat. "I see Mark waving at me. See you two later." She gave Clem another warning look that said, *Behave yourself!* and left.

"Were you really talking about me?" Luke asked. He was no longer smiling, but his green eyes were filled with amusement . . . and something else.

Something that made a delicious shudder snake its way down Clem's spine. "What do you think?"

"I think—" he lowered his voice "—that you are one sexy lady."

Clem swallowed. Usually she had no problem with snappy comebacks, but at that moment words deserted her.

He laughed softly. "I'll bet it's not often you're speechless."

"You just took me off guard, that's all," Clem finally managed to say.

His eyes said he knew that wasn't all. He raised his glass to his lips and took a swallow.

"I, uh, was just on my way out to the kitchen to say hello to our host. Have you met Bradley yet?"

"No, but I'd like to."

"Well, come on, I'll introduce you."

Clem told her heart and her stomach to settle down as she led the way into the big country kitchen. Bradley, looking solid and handsome in a dark suit, stood to one side of the restaurant-sized stove. Rita, the Strattons' housekeeper, was putting the finishing touches to a steaming pot of paella.

Bradley looked up as Clem and Luke approached. "Clem!" he said. His eyes lit up in delight.

Clem had always had a warm, fuzzy spot in her heart for Bradley. He was one of the most unaffected, plain-speaking, *sweet* people of the world, as friendly as a puppy and as good-hearted and generous a person as you'd ever want to meet. Nearly twenty years older than Annie, who like Clem was thirty-one, he had two grown sons and a grown daughter, all of whom adored him and had, after initial resistance, taken Annie into their hearts, too.

"Hi, Bradley," Clem greeted him. After they'd hugged, she turned to Luke. "This is Luke Taylor, Mark's older brother."

The two men shook hands and sized each other up. What they saw must have pleased them, for they immediately fell into a comfortable conversation.

"This is quite a place you've got here," Luke observed. "How many acres do you have?"

"Just over six thousand."

Luke whistled.

While Bradley told Luke more about the Stratton Ranch, Clem said hello to Rita. After a few minutes Bradley remarked, "I'd better get on out there and see to my guests before Annie comes after me with a whip."

The three of them joined the others in the huge L-shaped living room, dining room combination. Clem decided she wanted a glass of the champagne punch and headed for the dining room table. She didn't know Luke had followed her until he spoke. "I've been watching Channel 10 all week, but I haven't seen you once," he said.

Clem sipped at her punch and eyed him over the top of the crystal glass, trying not to let him see how pleased she was by his disclosure. "I've been working on a story all week. It'll probably air Monday."

"What kind of story?"

They moved away from the table and walked slowly back into the living room, then stood in one corner. "Oh, it's just one of those in-depth kind of things about discipline or the lack thereof in our schools." She made a face. "Not real news at all."

His smile was amused. "I know. You'd like to be covering something important, like wars."

"Yes, I would. Of course, I know that's not possible right now. After all, Houston doesn't have uprisings and wars. But at the very least, I'd like to cover *news.*"

"Like what?"

"Well, like the Spinosa trial or the Davison investigation." Theresa Spinosa had been accused of having her parents killed in a particularly grisly way and all because they had disapproved of her life-style and threatened to cut her off without a cent of their considerable fortune. Gene Davison was a highly placed city official indicted for taking construction kickbacks.

Luke nodded. "Guess I can't blame you for that. Those are two hot stories right now."

"Yes," Clem agreed glumly. "But my boss is a real Neanderthal. He doesn't believe women can handle stories like that. We get puff pieces and in-depth looks." She sighed. "It's really frustrating, especially when I've been with Channel 10 longer than several of the male reporters who've gotten better assignments for years. It's discrimination, plain and simple."

"Have you talked to your boss about the way you feel?"

"More times than I can count."

"And?"

"And he says I'm too inexperienced to cover stories like the Spinosa trial or the Davison indictment. But how will I ever *get* experience if he won't give me a chance?" She drank more of her punch. "If I could just come up with some kind of scoop, something that would knock his socks off, he'd *have* to pay attention to me."

"Like what?"

She shrugged. "I've got a couple of ideas I'm working on."

He nodded thoughtfully.

Just then Rita and the maid hired for the evening began bringing in the food, and people lined up. One of Clem's cousins walked up and asked her about a mutual friend, and Luke, smiling and saying, "We'll talk again later," walked off to join some of the men.

For the next hour or so Clem ate and talked and drank more punch.

About ten o'clock Annie clapped her hands and called, "Okay, gather round, everyone. Mark and Miranda are going to open their gifts."

While Mark and Miranda opened gifts, Clem did maid-of-honor duties by recording all the gifts and their various donors in Miranda's wedding book. Several times, when she looked up, she found Luke studying her. When their gazes connected he would smile, and she'd smile back. Each time, she tried to remember why it was she'd thought she wasn't interested in him, but her reasons seemed to have faded, or maybe they had never been valid to start with.

All she knew was that she liked him more and more all the time. And even if Miranda *hadn't* revealed Luke's interest, Clem would have known how he felt. The way he looked at her would have told her.

When all the presents were opened and duly recorded, Luke walked over and helped Mark stack them all near the door where they'd be carried out to Mark's car later. Then Luke headed in her direction again.

"Did you drive tonight?" he asked.

Clem's heart skipped. "No. I rode with Vanessa and Tommy."

"Would you like to ride back to Houston with me?"

Clem swallowed. Here it was. Decision time. She knew the smartest thing she could do was refuse. Luke Taylor was simply too attractive. Not the kind of guy you could easily walk away from. Definitely the kind of guy who, if he walked away from you, would probably leave a battered heart behind.

"I'd love to," she said.

Chapter Four

"It worked," Miranda said, dancing a little jig. "They left together!"

Mark grimaced. "Jeez, I hope this doesn't backfire. What if they compare notes?"

"Oh, they won't! After all, it's not the kind of thing you can say to someone else, is it?" She stopped dancing and struck a pose. "My sister says you've got a crush on me," she mimicked, laughing and shaking her head. "Can you picture Clem saying that? I don't *think* so."

"Yeah, I guess you're right." But Mark still felt uneasy. If he were Luke, and he found out about his brother's trickery, he would not be a happy camper.

Miranda slid her arms around him. "Quit worrying, honey. All we did was encourage them to do what they wanted to do, anyway."

Slowly Mark nodded. He guessed Miranda was right, about that point, anyway, and if he'd had any doubts, all he would've had to do was see the way Luke made a beeline for Clem the moment she walked into the Stratton house tonight to know which way the wind blew. If Luke hadn't been genuinely interested, he would have run like hell—in the other direction.

"We've done our part," Miranda declared happily. "Now the rest is up to them."

"Amen," Mark said.

Clem couldn't believe how easy it was to be with Luke. Or how easy it was to talk to him. She liked the fact that she could poke fun at him, or at men in general, and he didn't get all hot and bothered. He just poked fun right back.

Take his car, for instance.

When they'd walked outside and Luke had led the way to his car, Clem had been surprised to see it was a conservative dark gray four-door Honda Accord. "Somehow I pictured you driving a bright red Corvette or a big four-wheel-drive Bronco," she said.

Luke chuckled. "I got past the Bronco stage by the time I turned thirty." He unlocked the passenger door and helped her in. Even that simple touch caused a flutter in her chest.

"What about the Corvette stage? Isn't owning a sports car a rite of passage for men?" she asked after he'd gotten in on the driver's side.

"Like a Jeep is a rite of passage for aspiring war correspondents?" he quipped, fastening his seat belt and giving her a sidelong smile.

After a second she grinned and said, "Touché."

"Back to your question. I prefer to spend my money on something that gives me pleasure, like my photography, or something that will give me a good return on my investment, like my house."

"I noticed you taking pictures at the picnic. You looked like you knew what you were doing."

He smiled. "That's because I studied photography in college."

"You did? Is that what you planned to do? Be a photographer?"

"Yes. And I still hope that someday I can devote full time to it." He started the car and turned onto the long driveway lined with towering pines, which led to the private road that would eventually take them to the main highway and Houston.

"When you retire, you mean?"

His gaze met hers briefly before he turned his attention back to the road. "No, not exactly. I'm hoping things will work out so that I can do it full-time in a couple of years."

"What things?" Clem asked without thinking. Immediately she realized it was kind of a nosy question, but she couldn't take it back.

He hesitated a moment, then said lightly, "This is actually a pretty boring subject. Let's talk about something else."

Clem shrugged. If he didn't want to discuss the subject, that was okay with her. "All right. Tell me about your house. Where do you live?"

"Off lower Memorial Drive near the Loop."

Clem gave an inward whistle. If he owned a house in that area, which was one of the priciest in Houston, that business of his had to be doing very well.

"Where do *you* live?" he asked.

"I'm near the Loop, too. I have an apartment off San Felipe."

"Close to the station, then."

"Yes, that was the idea." She grimaced. "Not that it's mattered. It's not like they're calling me in the middle of the night to cover some late-breaking story." She sighed. "Sorry. I didn't mean to get back on that subject."

"It's okay. I understand. We all need to blow off steam sometimes."

"Yeah, well, I've been doing too much of that lately. It's a surefire way to bore your friends."

"I don't think you could ever be boring." His laugh was soft and intimate in the close confines of the car. "Frustrating, maybe. Opinionated, definitely. A pain in the you-know-what, probably. But boring? Never."

Clem laughed, too. "I'm glad you appreciate my finer qualities. Now, why don't you tell me about your business. Miranda says it's a security company?"

"Yes. We provide security and surveillance services. We have both personal and corporate accounts, but the corporate business is what really put us on the map."

"How'd you get into the security business if you started out wanting to be a photographer?"

"Well, my father was a cop, and he always wanted to have a business of his own, but he had seven kids to support, so he couldn't do anything about it. And then my grandfather died, and my father inherited some money, so he quit the force and took a chance. Unfortunately, six months later he died of a heart attack."

"Oh, how awful."

"Yes. He was only forty-two. Anyway, even though I knew absolutely nothing about the security business, I couldn't just let it fold, much less let my mother and younger brothers and sister starve. All of my parents' savings, as well as the inheritance from my grandfather, had been plowed into the company. So I quit school and took over the company. It was touch and go for a while, but I was lucky enough to hire a couple of good people who taught me a lot."

"And the company's become very successful."

"We've been fortunate, yes."

Clem knew it took more than luck to make a success of a business, especially one that employed quite a few people, as Luke's did. It took sacrifice and dedication and hard work. Lots of hard work.

"How old were you when your father died?"

"Twenty-two."

"How old are you now?"

"Are you always this nosy?" he countered.

She grinned. "Always. After all, I'm a reporter. I get paid to be nosy."

"I'll be thirty-nine next month. How old are you?"

"Thirty-one." They drifted into silence and Clem thought about what he'd said. "That's a lot of responsibility for a twenty-two-year-old to assume," she said after a while.

"I did what needed to be done."

She could hear in his voice that he wanted to drop the subject. She lightened her tone. "Okay, so now I know about your work. What do you do for fun?"

He smiled. "I don't have a lot of leisure time, but I do try to work out a few times a week. And, of course, there's always my photography. What do you do for fun?"

She shrugged. "Oh, I don't know. Normal stuff. I work out and I play pool and I go to movies and, you know, just stuff."

"You play pool?"

"Yes. Why do you say it that way?"

"I've never known a woman who played pool."

"That is such a sexist remark!"

He chuckled. "Sorry."

"You don't sound sorry at all." Honestly! Just when she was starting to think he might be different, he had to go and show his stripes.

"I really am sorry," he said contritely. "That *was* a sexist remark. It won't happen again."

"See that it doesn't," Clem retorted, slightly mollified.

"So where do you play?"

"At Big Ed's. It's a neighborhood ice house where I kind of hang out."

"Maybe we could have a game sometime."

"I play for blood," she warned.

"Now, how did I know that?" His voice was gently teasing.

She laughed. Maybe he was okay after all. "I also play for money."

"Of course." A heartbeat later he added, "How about Monday night? Are you busy?"

Clem swallowed. "No."

"Well, then, I challenge you to a couple of games of pool."

"You're on." Her pleasure in the evening deepened, bringing with it a keen edge of anticipation. This man would be a worthy adversary, both in the game of pool and in the more complicated man-woman game they had just begun.

For the rest of the way home they talked lightly, comfortably, with a teasing banter that Clem enjoyed more than she'd enjoyed anything in a long time. It seemed only minutes later when he pulled in to her apartment complex, but a glance at the clock on the dash told Clem it was past midnight.

"You can just let me out here," she suggested when her building came into view.

"I'll walk you to your door," he said firmly.

Clem didn't protest, which was odd for her. Normally she would insist she could walk to her door alone. She even waited for him to come around and open her door, something she never did. Companionably silent, they climbed to the second floor and walked to her door.

She turned to face him. The light from a nearby lamp cast interesting shadows across his face. "Thanks," she said. Her heart was beating a little too fast as she wondered if he would kiss her. Suddenly she wanted him to. Very much.

"You're very welcome."

"I, uh, I'd ask you in, but the place is a mess...."
Oh, shut up, Clem! She always talked too much when
she was nervous.

He placed his hands on her shoulders.

She shivered. His warm hands against her bare skin
caused chillbumps up and down her arms.

"How do you feel about kissing on a first date?" he
asked softly.

"*Is* this a first date?"

In answer he just smiled.

She licked her lips. "I, uh, don't have any rules one
way or the other." Oh, why couldn't she have thought
of something really clever to say?

His smile broadened. "Good," he whispered. He
lowered his head, and she raised her face to meet his.

Oh, wow, she thought for the second time that night
as his lips grazed hers, then settled more firmly. She
sighed as his hands slid down her arms, then pulled her
closer. When he deepened the kiss, something skyrocketed inside her, zigging and zagging through her
body.

He slowly broke the kiss.

They looked at each other for a long moment. Then
he said softly, "Where's your key?"

Clem wordlessly handed it to him, and he opened her
door. Just before she went in, he lifted her chin and
kissed her softly.

"Sweet dreams," he murmured.

Clem knew her dreams would be erotic rather than
sweet, but she decided it might be wise to keep that
thought to herself.

After she went inside she stood at her window and watched him leave. She couldn't remember the last time she'd felt this excited about a man. Maybe she'd *never* felt this excited about a man.

Suddenly the future looked more interesting than it had looked for a long time. Now, if only she could get things squared away with her career, she'd be the happiest woman in the world.

"Come on, Raymond," said Clem on Monday morning. "Don't ask me to interview a bunch of dancing teachers about the benefits of ballet training for athletes."

Raymond Tobias, the news director for Channel 10, and Clem's boss, raised his eyebrows. "It wasn't a request, Bennelli. It was an order."

Clem could almost feel the smoke coming out of her ears. She knew her blood pressure had probably skyrocketed up to the two hundred mark. If she hadn't been trying to persuade her pigheaded boss that she was just as capable, professional and tough as a man, she would have stamped her foot and screamed. *When* was Raymond going to realize that her intelligence and talent were completely wasted on these inane puff pieces?

She counted to ten. She would not lose her temper. She would be reasonable, logical and calm. "Raymond," she said reasonably, logically and calmly, "I have fulfilled every assignment you've given me. On time. Clean. Ready to go. Right?"

Raymond eyed her over his glasses, which normally sat at half-mast on his larger-than-normal nose. "Right."

"And I haven't complained...."

He smiled.

"Well, not much," she conceded. "But all along you've known that I thought eventually, when you realized I could handle it, you'd give me something meatier. Something *important.*"

He pursed his lips.

"Well, I'm ready. I'm more than ready. Give the dance thing to Monica. She loves stuff like that. Let me do the story on Gene Davison."

"Oh, come on, get real, Bennelli. Next to the Spinosa murders, that's the biggest story to hit Houston this year."

"I know. That's why I want it."

Raymond shook his head. "You're not ready for anything like that. I need someone experienced to cover that story."

"I'll never be ready for anything like that if you don't give me a chance!" *Careful, careful, don't raise your voice, he'll accuse you of being too emotional.*

He was still shaking his head.

"Come on, Raymond. I can do it. Let me do it."

"I've already assigned that story to Charles."

Clem gritted her teeth. She loathed Charles Frey. He got every important story, and he wasn't *half* as good as she was. His copy always needed extensive editing, and half the time he failed to follow up on the simplest leads. Yet Raymond continued to favor him over Clem. And it was just because she was a woman.

"I'm not doing the dance teacher story." If he wanted to fire her, let him. She had to take a stand sometime.

He considered her stony face for a long moment. "Tell you what. I'll give Monica that story. If you want to show me your stuff, do it by getting an interview with Judge Pollock."

"Oh, come on, Raymond. That's not fair." Judge Fred Pollock was the presiding judge for the Spinosa case, which was due to go to trial this week, and he had refused all interviews.

"What's not fair about it?" Raymond asked innocently.

"You know damn well what's not fair about it. Judge Pollock isn't going to talk to me. He's made his position perfectly clear. No interviews. Not until the trial's over."

"If you're as good as you claim, getting him to change his mind ought to be a piece of cake."

Clem felt like throwing something at him. "Gee, thanks a lot, Raymond," she said sweetly. "You're a real prince."

Raymond smiled. "Thank you. And would you please close the door on your way out?"

Clem fumed for the rest of the day Monday. She was so frustrated. Today's incident was so typical of what it was like to work for someone like Raymond. It made no difference that she'd done everything she was supposed to do since coming to Channel 10: worked hard, played by the rules, kept her nose clean. Raymond simply refused to recognize her worth.

And at this rate, he was never going to.

Just look at what had happened today. She'd made a reasonable request, and he'd given her an unreasonable assignment. Something was going to have to change. She was going to have to make sure something changed.

But what? And how?

As Clem drove home that night, she continued to weigh all the possibilities open to her. Bitching and complaining were getting her nowhere.

Maybe it was time to find another job.

She sighed as she braked for a stop sign.

She didn't want another job. She'd invested so much time and energy into her position at Channel 10. Going somewhere else would mean starting over. Shoot, if she went somewhere else, she wanted to be going to the network, to a bigger job with more responsibility.

She remembered the smirk on Raymond's face as he'd told her to get an interview with Judge Pollock. Oh, if she could only pull it off. She could just imagine how he'd react if she were to march triumphantly into his office, waving a videotaped interview in his face. Clem grinned. Raymond would be speechless. And then he'd *have* to give her better assignments.

But how could she get Judge Pollock to grant her an interview when no one else had had any luck?

"So now I've got to figure out a way to get an interview with Judge Pollock," Clem said. She and Luke were sitting at one of the outside tables at Big Ed's. They'd played five games of pool, and she'd won three, as well as a nice chunk of Luke's money. She'd also talked nonstop, insulted him several times and argued with him about every other thing he said.

He'd had a wonderful time.

They had just ordered cheeseburgers and beer and were waiting for their food, and she had been telling him about her confrontation with her boss earlier that day.

With each passing minute he was more and more convinced that he'd made the right decision when he'd impulsively asked her out. Earlier today he'd started to feel guilty about leaving work early, because he was so swamped, but then he'd thought, why shouldn't he have *some* semblance of a normal life? He might not be able to figure out a way to get out from under the company altogether, but he sure as heck could leave the office at a reasonable hour. After all, his brothers and sister did. And now, looking at Clem, enjoying her company and her conversation, *relaxing* for a change, he was very glad he'd invited her out tonight.

She was fun to watch. She looked sexy as all get-out in her tight jeans and red-and-white-striped T-shirt, with her face all flushed with exertion and victory and passion over her job. "Maybe I could help you out," he said when she finally stopped for a breath.

She stared at him, her big blue eyes looking even bigger and bluer than normal.

"I did a security job for the judge once and . . ." He shrugged. "I think he might be willing to do me a favor."

"Luke, *really?*"

He smiled. "Yes, really."

"Oh, God, Raymond would pee his pants if I came in with an interview."

Luke laughed. He *did* love the way Clem refused to censor her words.

She rubbed her hands together gleefully. "He'd *have* to give me better assignments. Because if he didn't, I'd haul him before the EEOC."

"Would you?"

"Well, I'd *like* to," she said, frowning. "I could *threaten* to."

"Don't count your chickens yet. The judge might refuse."

She grinned. "I can't imagine anyone refusing you anything."

Suddenly the atmosphere was charged with sexual tension. It was almost a palpable thing, arcing across the table and igniting all those damned male hormones again. Luke's gaze slid to Clem's mouth—those wonderfully kissable lips. He swallowed, thinking about that sizzler of a kiss they'd shared Saturday night. If they hadn't been in such a public place he'd have gotten up and yanked her out of her chair and kissed her until she begged for mercy.

Her eyes told him she knew exactly what he was thinking. Her rapid breathing told him she wanted him the same way he wanted her. He wondered how she felt about sex on a second date.

Down, boy, down, he chastised himself. *Don't jump into anything. Just because she's fun, and just because you're attracted to her, doesn't change things. Remember, she's your future sister-in-law's sister. Also remember that you have no interest in permanent commitment of any kind. Remember that this could be, and probably is, dangerous territory.*

He looked away from her mouth, which was the most dangerous territory of all right now.

Just then their number was called, meaning their food was ready. *Saved by the bell,* Luke thought. "I'll go get the food."

She nodded, and once again something shimmered in the air between them.

Luke took a deep breath as he walked away. He knew he needed to tread carefully. Extremely carefully. Before he made any moves, he had to think of the consequences. My God, didn't he have enough complications in his life?

By the time he took the food to the table he'd gotten his thoughts and his hormones under control again, and he told himself they would stay under control. He would make no rash moves. In fact, any moves at all would have to be initiated by her.

Later, after they'd eaten their juicy burgers and had drunk a couple of bottles of beer apiece, they walked back to her apartment, which was only a few blocks away. Sometime between the time they left the ice house and the time they reached her complex, Luke decided that even if Clem acted willing, he was not going to take her to bed tonight.

It was simply too soon.

She was simply too attractive.

He needed more time to think about all the ramifications of a relationship with her.

So he would cool it when they got to her door. One kiss. That's all.

Easier said than done, he thought as Clem willingly came into his arms and lifted her face. *Much easier said than done.* The trouble was, she felt so good, so right, in his arms. He loved the fact that she was tall and strong, that there was nothing clingy or twittery about her. He couldn't stand clingy, twittery females.

Even so, she was definitely all woman.

So he didn't hold to his vow. He kissed her several times, each kiss more hungry and demanding than the last. Finally, breathing hard, they separated.

"Wow," Clem said softly.

"You can say that again," he whispered against her forehead.

"Wow...."

He laughed and knew that if she gave him any kind of signal that she wanted him to come inside, all his good intentions would go down the drain.

She didn't.

She just sighed and said, "I'd better get in. Early day tomorrow."

He nodded. Although he knew this was the wisest course, he couldn't help feeling regretful. He kissed the tip of her nose. "I'll call Judge Pollock tomorrow morning."

She smiled, and her eyes looked luminous in the moonlight. "I have complete faith in you."

Luke felt a twinge of uneasiness. He hoped he was doing the right thing.

Clem leaned against the door after Luke left. Her face felt hot. Inside, she felt all mushy and soft and needy. Oh, God, what was wrong with her? When she was with Luke, all of her good resolutions seemed to fly out the window. It was madness to get involved with this man. She liked him too darned much! So why was she doing it?

"Clementine Bennelli, you're in big trouble," she said aloud. "Very big trouble."

Chapter Five

Luke eyed the phone for a long moment before picking it up and dialing the number. Several times since he'd made the offer to call Judge Pollock, he'd wished he hadn't. He knew it wasn't wise to get any more deeply involved with Clem, but it was too late to back out now.

"Judge Pollock's chambers," said the woman who answered the phone.

"This is Luke Taylor, Taylor Security. Is Judge Pollock around?"

"No, sir. He's out to lunch. Would you like to leave a message?"

Luke left word that he'd like the judge to call him, then hung up. A few seconds later his sister knocked on his office door.

Although Rebecca was not the youngest in the family, as the only girl among six brothers she had always seemed so. Sometimes it was hard to believe she was almost thirty. In Luke's mind she'd always be his baby sister.

"Hey, Luke, got a minute?" she asked.

He smiled. "For you? Always. Come on in. Sit down."

He watched her with pleasure as she sat in one of the chairs flanking his desk and crossed her legs. As always, she looked businesslike but attractive in her cream-colored blouse and dark skirt, which were a perfect complement to her creamy complexion and thick, dark blond hair and green eyes. The green eyes were a Taylor family trait—all but two of the seven siblings had them.

As he had so many times before, he wondered why Rebecca wasn't married yet. He knew she'd had her share of suitors, but nothing permanent ever seemed to come of them. When he'd teased her about it once, saying maybe she was like him and would remain single all of her life, she'd laughed and said, "Hope not. The trouble is, I'm picky. And so far no one's come close to meeting my standards."

"What's on your mind?" he said now.

"Well, there's something I've been wanting to talk to you about for a while now."

There was an apprehensive edge to her voice, which gave Luke an uneasy feeling. Was something wrong? "Sounds serious."

"It is serious, at least to me. I, uh..." She took a deep breath. "Luke, would you consider buying out my share of the company?"

Luke couldn't have been more surprised if she'd socked him in the stomach. Of all the things he might have imagined her saying, this was the absolute furthest from his mind. "I don't understand," he finally said. "Are you having financial problems?"

"No, no, it's not that. Well, I guess I should clarify. Yes, I do need money, but it's not because I'm in any kind of *trouble.*" She met his gaze evenly. "The thing is, Luke, I want out."

"You want out? What do you mean?"

She sighed. "Just that. I want out of the company." She paused, looked down at her lap for a moment, then looked up again. She seemed to be choosing her words carefully. "It's nothing against you. It's nothing against the company, either. Not really. It's just that I have no interest in my job. It bores me silly. I've been thinking about this a lot lately, and you know, I've come to the conclusion that life is too short to spend the majority of it in a job that gives you no pleasure."

For a long moment Luke was speechless. Her words reverberated in his mind. *I have no interest in my job. It bores me. Life is too short to spend it in a job that gives you no pleasure.* No kidding! he felt like saying. How the hell do you think *I've* felt all these years? I certainly never intended to spend my life pushing papers or working in a field that was our father's dream instead of mine.

"Say something, Luke," she implored.

He gave himself a mental shake. "Sorry. You just took me by surprise. I never knew you felt this way."

"I know. No one did."

"If you leave here, what do you intend to do?"

"Go back to school," she replied eagerly. "Get my degree in advertising. Then, hopefully, go to work for one of the agencies here."

Luke rubbed his chin. "It's going to be tough getting along without you if you leave." Rebecca was his office manager, and under their accountant's guidance she did the major portion of the bookkeeping.

"Oh, I'm sure you can easily replace me," she said. "After all, this really is a good place to work, and my job is an excellent one. Someone else would probably love it. But don't worry. I'll stay long enough to get someone trained. I wouldn't just walk out on you. Besides, I don't intend to enroll in school until the fall. I want to be free to enjoy the summer. I had hoped, though, to be through here by the end of June so I could have a couple of months to just relax and maybe do some traveling."

With every word she was rubbing salt in the wound. Luke would kill to have two months off to relax and travel and work on his photography, but how could he? As it was now, he was always swamped, always behind. He could just imagine the mess he'd come back to if he were to indulge himself the way Rebecca wanted to indulge herself.

She smiled. "Well? What do you say? Will you buy me out?"

He knew the answer she expected. He even knew that he would probably end up giving it to her. But he couldn't help the resentment slowly creeping into his psyche. When was it going to be *his* turn?

Just then the phone at his elbow rang, and he said, "I need to look at some numbers before I can give you an answer. Can we talk about this later?" When she nodded her agreement, he picked up the phone. "Luke Taylor."

"Luke. This is Fred Pollock. My secretary said you called me."

"Yes, hello, Judge Pollock." Rebecca mouthed a goodbye and left, shutting the door behind her. "Thanks for calling me back so fast," he said to the judge.

"What can I do for you?" Judge Pollock inquired briskly.

Luke pushed the conversation with Rebecca to the back of his mind. He would think about that problem later. "Well," he said, "I have this friend . . ."

"Luke!" Clem exclaimed, then realized where she was and dropped her voice so no one at the surrounding desks could overhear her. "Do you mean it? Judge Pollock said yes? He'll give me an interview?"

"Yep. He agreed."

"God, that's wonderful! How can I *ever* thank you?"

He chuckled, the sound soft and intimate and faintly erotic coming over the telephone wire. "I'm sure we can think of something. . . ."

She laughed, happiness rushing through her in a great flood. Life was good. And it was getting better every day! She couldn't believe how just a few days ago she'd been so down in the dumps. Now the future looked promising and bright, and a lot of it was due to Luke. And to think how she'd maligned him at first.

He really was a decent man, and even though he sometimes reverted to type and made sexist remarks, he'd certainly made amends today!

"Judge Pollock said to be waiting outside his chambers at seven-thirty tomorrow morning. Can you make it?" he asked.

"Are you kidding? If he told me to be on Mars at three o'clock this afternoon, I'd make it!"

"Good. I'll be curious to know how it goes."

"I'll call you tomorrow as soon as the interview is over."

"Okay, great. Good luck with the interview. Pollock's a tough old bird. He might give you a hard time."

"I can handle it."

"Is there anything you *can't* handle?"

"Nope. I'm a tough bird, too."

He chuckled again. "You know, I almost feel sorry for the judge."

After calling Clem, Luke tried to settle back down to work, but Rebecca's request and his negative feelings about it kept interfering with his concentration.

Then, just as he'd finally managed to settle into a lengthy report, his brother Paul appeared at his door.

"Luke, hey, listen, I've got a conflict, and I can't go to Austin tomorrow," he said, walking in and plopping down in one of the chairs flanking Luke's desk.

Luke tamped down the mild irritation he felt at Paul's barging in without even asking if Luke was busy. "Tell me you're kidding me."

"No, hey, I really can't go. Jennifer's got a dance recital tomorrow night, and I forgot about it when I said I could go. You know Molly. She'll kill me if I'm not there."

"Come on, Paul, the world won't topple off its axis if you miss one of Jennifer's recitals. You've *got* to go to Austin. There's no one else."

Paul shrugged. "I'm sorry, but I can't. We'll just have to cancel."

"If we cancel, we might as well kiss the contract goodbye, you know that."

"You could go."

"Me?" Luke said. "I'm snowed under. I've got to get the Sunnygrove Apartment proposal ready, I've got two other bids waiting for me to look at them and there are at least five reports that need to be written." He grimaced. "Not to mention the reviews I was supposed to do last week."

"Maybe you should hire an assistant," Paul suggested.

"Maybe you or Mark or John could take over some of this paperwork," Luke countered.

Paul put his hands up as if warding off an attack. "I can't speak for Mark or John, but I'm not interested in management. I like having a personal life too much. I sure as heck don't want to be stuck working sixty hours a week like you do."

"Did you ever stop to think that maybe I don't want to work sixty hours a week, either?"

Paul seemed taken aback for a few seconds, and then he chuckled. "Oh, come on, Luke, we all know you live and breathe this business."

And then, before Luke even had a chance to form an answer, Paul stood. "I gotta get going. I promised Molly I'd pick Jennifer up at school. Sorry about tomorrow." He walked off whistling.

Luke buried his head in his hands and wondered what his family would do if one day he just packed up and took off and never came back.

Jason Ruggerio, Clem's favorite cameraman, met her in the station parking lot at six forty-five the following morning as prearranged.

"Did you check out a van?" she asked as she strode up to him.

"Yep." His dark eyes twinkled.

"Did Glenna give you any trouble?"

"Nope."

"What did you tell her?"

"That I had a hot tip. What else?"

"You didn't mention my name, did you?"

"Hey, Bennelli, do you think I'm stupid? Huh? Huh?"

He made a dumb face, and Clem laughed.

Thirty minutes later they pulled in to a parking slot right in front of the courthouse. "You must live right," Jason said.

Clem grinned.

"How'd you wangle this interview, anyway?" Jason asked as she helped him remove the video camera equipment.

"I have my sources."

Jason nodded. "Raymond's going to have a stroke."

"I know. Isn't it *great?*"

A few minutes later the two of them stood waiting outside Judge Pollock's chambers. On the dot of seven-thirty the bushy-haired judge, whom Clem recognized from pictures that had appeared in the newspaper, strode down the hall toward them.

Clem's heart did a little jig of excitement. *Hail Mary, full of grace, please keep me from falling flat on my face,* she prayed, using her own personal litany. As the judge came closer, she smiled. "Judge Pollock? I'm Clem Bennelli from Channel 10, and this is Jason Ruggerio, my cameraman." She held out her hand.

The judge nodded, his dark eyes sharp as they appraised her. Ignoring her hand, he withdrew a key from his pocket and opened the door. "Come in, please."

Clem grimaced at Jason behind the judge's back, then took a deep breath and, gesturing to Jason to follow, walked in after Judge Pollock.

The judge pointed at several chairs on one side of the square room, then walked toward a large desk piled with papers and law books. He opened a closet behind the desk and removed a black robe. After removing his suit jacket and replacing it with the robe, he sat behind the desk. "I'll give you twenty minutes, no more," he said brusquely.

"Okay, no problem," Clem replied. "Is that the setting you want? Your desk?"

"What's wrong with it?"

"Nothing. Nothing at all. I just wanted to be sure." She gave him a brief run-through of the way the interview would progress, then inclined her head in Jason's direction, and he moved to the side of her where he'd have an unobstructed view of the judge. He turned on the camera, swiveling it in Clem's direction first.

Clem opened her notebook. "I'm standing here in Judge Fred Pollock's chambers. In less than an hour the Spinosa trial will begin. It's one of the most notorious cases to ever come to trial in Houston, and today we're going to talk to Judge Pollock, the presiding judge." She turned to face the judge. "Good morning, Judge Pollock."

"Good morning." He didn't smile.

Luke was right. He's definitely a tough old bird, thought Clem. "I know you're not pleased with all the media coverage of this case, so I really appreciate your consenting to talk to me."

"Yes, I'm a busy man, so let's get on with it."

"Do you feel the heavy media attention this case has received might have compromised Theresa Spinosa's chances of getting a fair trial in Houston?"

His eyes narrowed. "Young lady, if I thought so, I'd have encouraged the prosecution to move for a change of venue."

Ohh-kay, Clem thought. "So you feel confident that Theresa Spinosa will receive a fair trial."

"Yes, I do." His dark eyes told her if she asked one more question he considered stupid, he would terminate the interview.

Clem glanced down at her notes. "You've had a great deal of experience with criminal trials. What's been the most interesting one you've presided over so far?" Clem held her breath. This question would make or break her interview. If the judge refused to talk about himself, Clem had nowhere else to go, because she knew there was no way he'd discuss any aspect of the Spinosa case.

Judge Pollock launched into a description of a famous case from about a dozen years earlier, and Clem let out her breath. She kept the flow going by interjecting questions. Gradually the questions became more general, then she segued into more pointed ones.

She ended with, "How long do you estimate the Spinosa trial will last?"

"Weeks, months, maybe." His gaze rose to the clock on the wall.

Clem knew the interview was over. She thanked him profusely, but he shrugged her thanks away. As she and Jason prepared to leave, the judge turned and said, "Tell that young man of yours we're even now." Then he smiled, and the smile transformed his face. "You can also tell him he's got good taste."

Clem never blushed, but she could feel her face heating up. "Th-thanks," she stammered. A friendly Judge Pollock was almost harder to take than a tough Judge Pollock.

"That young man of yours," Jason said under his breath as they made their escape. "You're a deep one, Bennelli. Who is he, and why haven't we heard about him?"

Clem gave him her don't-mess-with-me look. "The judge is wrong. It was just a friend who helped me get the interview, that's all."

Jason smiled. "Okay, if you don't want to tell me, I understand."

"Good. Because there's nothing to tell."

Four hours later, the interview edited and polished down to a clean four minutes, Clem strode into Raymond's office. She stopped in front of his desk and tossed the tape onto the pile of papers in front of him. "You wanted Judge Pollock. You got Judge Pollock." She told herself not to gloat, but she couldn't stop the grin spreading across her face, because Raymond looked just as stupefied and speechless as she'd pictured him looking.

When he finally recovered his composure, he said, "How'd you manage it, Bennelli?"

"Trade secret."

They eyed each other for several more moments. Then Raymond sighed. He tossed the tape back to her. "Play it for me."

She did.

Afterward he grudgingly said, "Congratulations. That's a fine piece."

"I know it." She waited.

After a few more pregnant seconds he added, "I'll assign Nick Slocum to another story. From now on, the Spinosa trial is yours."

Clem permitted herself a small smile of victory. "Thank you, Raymond. That means I'll need Jason for the duration."

He sighed again. "Done. Now Bennelli, would you please quit bothering me and get out of my office and let me get back to work?"

Clem managed not to skip or dance until she was safely out of Raymond's sight. Even then, she managed to keep her excitement confined to a murmured, "Yes, yes, *yes!*" as she punched the air.

For the rest of the day she was euphoric. If Luke had been there she would have tackled him and planted kisses all over his sexy face.

She couldn't wait to talk to him.

Luke drove to Austin very early Wednesday morning. He brought the most urgent of his paperwork with him because he was afraid the Austin job would take at least three days.

The first day at the client site passed quickly, and he had no time either to think about his dilemma regarding his increasingly strong desire to be free of the company and the pressures of his job or to think about Clem.

But Wednesday night, when he got back to his hotel, his thoughts again turned to Clem. Several times that evening he was tempted to call her to find out how the interview had gone. But he told himself to cool it. Calling her over the weekend was soon enough. He didn't want to send out any false signals. First he had to decide where they were going. *If* they were going, he amended.

He knew he had to come to some kind of decision about Clem soon. It was pure folly to continue seeing her unless he expected to take the relationship further.

He sighed, propping his feet up on the motel bed. This thing between him and Clem—it was dangerous because it was so intense and so undeniable. Even if Mark hadn't told him about Clem's interest in him, he would have known it. How could he not know it? Their awareness of each other fairly crackled when they were together.

Why had he had to meet Clem now, when his life was in such turmoil? It was bad enough that he seemed to be at some kind of crossroads where he needed to make some hard life decisions, but to have the added complication of a new relationship was stupid—wasn't it? And then, to top everything off, Clem was Miranda's sister.

Luke wondered what he should do. Either he should stop seeing Clem completely, or—if he didn't want to do that—maybe he should just lay all his cards on the table. Tell Clem how upside-down his life was and how he felt about permanent entanglements.

And who knows?

She might feel the same way.

Certainly her life-style didn't lend itself to any kind of permanent relationship.

Maybe he should say, *Look, Clem, I am very attracted to you, but I knew long ago that marriage isn't for me. I've got enough responsibilities, enough people depending on me. I don't need more.*

The more he thought about it, the more he liked the idea. But this wasn't the kind of thing to say on the phone. This kind of thing had to be done face-to-face.

He would talk to her this weekend.

That decided, he dug his paperwork out of his briefcase and settled down to work.

Clem was disappointed when she called Luke's office on Wednesday afternoon and found out he'd had to go out of town unexpectedly. Her disappointment abated somewhat, though, when his secretary added, "He said to tell you he'd call you this weekend, Miss Bennelli."

At least he'd thought of her, Clem told herself as she hung up. Then she got mad at herself.

And why do you care whether he thinks of you or not?

Well, I don't really *care*, but no woman likes to think a man will just completely *forget* about her.

Uh-huh. Tell me another one.

Clem told her inner voice to drop dead, but she couldn't completely banish the little thrill of excitement every time she thought about seeing Luke again.

On Friday evening Miranda had her final fitting for her wedding dress. She had asked Clem to meet her at the shop at seven o'clock.

Clem was tired. It had been a long day in court. There were so many gawkers and spectators that she hadn't been able to get a seat in the courtroom and had stood in the back for most of the day. She guessed she should count herself lucky she'd gotten in, period. Getting back to the station had taken forever, too, in the Friday-afternoon traffic.

She arrived at the bridal shop at a few minutes past seven in a state of bleary-eyed exhaustion. When she entered, Miranda was already there, dressed in her wedding gown.

The funniest feeling slid through Clem's stomach as she gazed at her sister. Miranda looked radiant. The dress, a simple white satin trimmed in lace, accentuated her dark beauty. She smiled at Clem.

For the first time in her life Clem felt wistful, almost envious, knowing she'd never wear a dress like this one. But just as quickly she scoffed at herself for falling victim to that old fairy-tale fantasy her mother and sisters were always trying to feed her.

You're not cut out to be princess for a day, she reminded herself. Actually, the princess-for-a-day bit wasn't the problem. It was everything that went along with it. The sacrifice and the subjugation of her goals to someone else's. Remember that, she lectured herself. Anytime you feel envious, just remember that.

But the vision of Miranda stayed with her, and that night Clem even dreamed about her. Only in her dream, it was Clem in the beautiful satin dress walking down a long aisle to the strains of Mendelssohn's "Wedding March" from *Midsummer Night's Dream* with someone who looked suspiciously like Luke waiting at the other end.

The next morning, when she awakened and remembered the dream, she felt disturbed and uneasy.

She told herself the dream meant nothing. It was normal to get a little crazy and misty-eyed over a wedding. It certainly didn't mean Clem wanted to be in Miranda's shoes. Or that she wanted Luke as a husband.

You don't want to get married. Marriage would spoil everything. You have things to do, places to go. A commitment like marriage would make those things and places impossible.

She thought about her mother's life.

Her sisters' lives.

They all seemed happy enough, but their lives were so *boring,* so ordinary and predictable.

Clem didn't want boring and predictable. She didn't want PTA and a nine-to-five job and grocery shopping. She wanted excitement and challenge and travel. She wanted to make decisions based on what *she* wanted, not what someone else wanted.

She knew other people might consider her selfish. She preferred to think of herself as single-minded.

Throughout the day, as she researched the Spinosa case, reading through the reams of copy written about it and planning the way she would approach that week's coverage, she thought about her reaction to seeing Miranda in her wedding finery and the conclusions she'd drawn afterward.

By four o'clock, when she finally decided to head home, she had made a decision. If she planned to continue seeing Luke, they would have to get things straight between them. She would have to tell him how she felt and see how he felt.

Because no matter how much she liked him, no matter how much she wished she could keep seeing him, and no matter how sexually attracted to him she was—if he was looking for marriage, he'd better look elsewhere.

Chapter Six

If Clem had no other plans, she always ate Sunday dinner at her parents' house. This Sunday was no exception. In spite of the occasional grumbling to friends about "command performances," Clem enjoyed these family get-togethers, especially when she had something good to talk about.

That afternoon she was feeling particularly pleased with herself because her interview with Judge Pollock had made the six-o'clock and ten-o'clock news on Thursday. In addition, the interview had been picked up by the network feed and shown in dozens of other markets in Texas and the surrounding areas.

An old college friend of hers who now lived in Lafayette had called to say he'd seen her on the network affiliate there, and another friend in Dallas and one in Little Rock had E-mailed her their congratulations.

Added to all that, her co-workers at Channel 10 had been gratifyingly envious as well as complimentary about the job she'd done.

She was looking forward to her family's reaction. When she arrived at her parents' home in the Heights, where they'd lived ever since their marriage thirty-eight years earlier, her mother beamed at her. "I heard the news," she said, her blue eyes bright.

Clem preened a little bit.

"I'm so pleased," her mother continued as she slid the roaster out of the oven and placed it on a hot pad on the kitchen counter. Tantalizing smells permeated the kitchen.

Clem preened a bit more.

"So, what do you think of him?" Her mother lifted the lid on a pot that was simmering on the stove, stirred, then replaced the lid.

"Well, he's kind of a tough old guy, but he was pretty decent to me."

Her mother turned around, a frown marring her forehead. "He doesn't seem that old to me, and what do you mean, *pretty decent to you?*"

"He's at least sixty-five, maybe older," Clem answered. She stuck her fingers into the salad bowl sitting on the counter and extracted a cherry tomato. "Umm," she said, popping it into her mouth.

Her mother's expression was now incredulous. "Luke? He couldn't be more than forty, if that."

"Luke? Who's talking about Luke?"

"I was," her mother said. "Weren't you?"

"No!" Clem declared indignantly. "I was talking about Judge Pollock."

"Judge Pollock? Why were you talking about him?"

"Oh, for Pete's sake," Clem said in exasperation. "Don't you watch Channel 10? Didn't you see my interview with the judge?"

"Yes."

"Well, *that's* why I thought you meant the judge. That interview was a real coup, Ma. I'm the only reporter in town who's gotten the judge to talk to the media. I'm pretty proud of it, and I certainly thought my *parents* would be proud of it!"

Her mother's face slid into its long-suffering mode. "Well, of course I'm proud of your interview. I just wasn't thinking about Judge Pollock right this minute."

"Then why on earth did you say you'd heard the news? And that you were pleased?"

"I meant I heard the news that you're dating Luke Taylor." She smiled happily. "That's why I'm pleased. I had a long talk with him at the picnic, you know, and I thought he was very nice. And perfect for you."

Clem counted to ten before speaking, because she really did love her mother, and she didn't want to say anything she'd be sorry for later. "First of all, I'm not *dating* Luke. I only went out with him once. Secondly, who told you I was dating him, anyway?" And how in the hell had anyone even known about Monday night? Clem certainly hadn't told anyone. Had Luke?

"Now, honey," her mother soothed, "don't get upset. Miranda and I were just talking—"

"Well, I don't appreciate people talking behind my back," Clem said stiffly.

"For heaven's sake, Clem, don't be so prickly."

"Prickly? I'm not prickly." Clem knew she was behaving badly, but she hated to think that they were all discussing her and her love life.

Her mother grinned. "If you were any more prickly, you'd be a rosebush."

"Ha, ha. Very funny."

"Well, it's true," her mother said mildly, not in the least disturbed by Clem's irritability.

"What's true?" asked Clem's brother Frank, who walked into the kitchen and opened the refrigerator.

"I was just telling your sister not to be so touchy," Clem's mother replied as she began to slice a loaf of French bread.

Frank, who at thirty-five was four years Clem's senior and a favorite of hers, grinned as he extracted a beer from the refrigerator and popped the top. "Our Clementine?" he said, winking at Clem. "Touchy? That's very difficult to believe."

Clem stuck her tongue out at him.

He grinned, walking over and putting his arm around her shoulders. "Hey, little sister, congratulations on snaring that interview with Judge Pollock. You did a great job."

Clem's irritation melted away under his warm praise. She beamed. "Thanks."

"What'd the famous Raymond have to say about it?" Frank asked.

"What *could* he say? He had to acknowledge that it was good work. And he *had* to give me a good assignment out of it, so now I'm on the Spinosa case for the duration."

Frank laughed. "How sweet it is...."

Later, over dinner, the subject of the interview came up again, and this time Clem couldn't have asked for more gratifying comments. Even the twins, normally not at all interested in news unless it was the kind that appeared on "Inside Edition" or "Hard Copy," congratulated her.

Valerie practically gushed, saying, "Gee, Clem, you sounded so *smart* in that interview, and are you *really* going to hear the entire *case?*" Her voice rose a couple of notches with each word.

"Thanks, and yes, I am," Clem answered.

"How'd you persuade the judge to talk to you, anyway, Clem?" her father asked. "I thought he hated the media."

"Oh, I have connections," she said. She ate some of her stuffed flank steak and hoped her father wouldn't press her further.

"Come on, tell us," her father persisted. "It's not a secret, is it?"

"Well, no...." Oh, shoot. She should have just told him to begin with. Now the disclosure of Luke's involvement would seem as if it was more important than it was. "Actually, Mark's brother arranged it for me."

Mark, who was having Sunday dinner with them, looked up. "My brother? Which brother? You mean Luke?" he said in disbelief. "How'd that happen?"

"Yes, I mean Luke." Clem willed herself not to blush. "I just happened to mention to him how my boss had challenged me to get the interview, and he very kindly offered his help." She nonchalantly ate some salad.

"Gee, that was *so-o-o* nice of him, wasn't it?" cooed Vanessa.

"It *was* nice," agreed Miranda.

Drop the subject, drop the subject, Clem willed them, resolutely not meeting anyone's eyes. She did not want to get into a discussion about Luke or her involvement with him.

Showing a surprising sensitivity, Clem's mother said, "Have you seen Theresa Spinosa yet, Clem?"

Clem gratefully launched into a description of the notorious defendant, and the subject of Luke wasn't brought up again until later when she and her sisters were helping their mother clean up the kitchen.

Miranda reintroduced the subject, saying, "Mark tells me Luke has been in Austin this week."

The remark had been addressed to Clem, so she nodded and said casually, "So I gathered." She picked a casserole dish out of the drainer and began drying it.

"Have you talked to him?"

"Nope." She kept her gaze trained on the casserole. She didn't think it was anyone's business that he'd left a message on her recorder yesterday saying he wouldn't be back in town until late today and he would call her tonight.

"Do you expect to talk to him?" Miranda persisted.

The silence spun out for long seconds as everyone waited for Clem to answer. Finally she looked up. Four pairs of blue eyes met hers. "Come on, you guys, gimme a break!"

They all grinned.

Then Vanessa said, "All I have to say is, if I wasn't already married, I'd give you a run for your money, Clem, 'cause I think Luke Taylor is absolutely the sexiest man alive...except for Tommy, of course." Tommy was Vanessa's husband. "Gee, just think," she added breathlessly, "if Clem married Luke, she and Miranda would be sisters-in-law!"

The others giggled, even Clem's mother, who certainly should have known better.

Clem threw her dish towel down on the counter. "Listen, let's get something straight. I've only gone out with Luke once. I don't know if I'll go out with him again. But I do know that even if I do, I am *not*, repeat *not*, going to marry him. I'm not going to marry anyone. Period. End of discussion."

Then she turned on her heel and huffily went off into the living room and the relative safety of her brothers' and father's and future brother-in-law's company.

Luke called as promised about eight o'clock Sunday night. "I saw your interview. They ran it on the affiliate station in Austin."

"They did?" Clem said delightedly.

"You did a fantastic job, Miss Bennelli. I congratulate you."

"Thanks." Pleasure warmed Clem's insides.

"So tell me all about it."

For the next fifteen minutes she did. She described the interview in detail, only omitting the remarks Judge Pollock had made to her at the end. Then she described the triumphant showdown with Raymond and its satisfying results.

"So you're covering the Spinosa case now?" he said when she finished. "That's great. That ought to go a long way toward getting you where you want to go."

"Yes, and I owe all of this to you. Thanks again, Luke. I won't forget it."

"See that you don't," he said, chuckling in that low, sexy way of his.

Something skittered through Clem, and she shivered.

"I'd like to see you again, Clem."

The skittery feeling intensified. "I'd like that, too."

"But the next few days are going to be really jam-packed. I'm more behind than ever because of the unexpected Austin trip, plus with the wedding coming up..."

"Hey, it's okay. Don't worry about it. I'm swamped myself."

"But I was thinking," he said. "How about if I pick you up on Friday and we go to the rehearsal and the rehearsal dinner together?"

"Okay. Sure. I'd like that."

"The rehearsal's at six, isn't it?"

"Yes."

"Then I'll pick you up about five-thirty."

"Great."

"I'm looking forward to it."

"Me, too."

Friday, she thought, after they'd hung up. Friday would either make or break their relationship. After Friday they would either become lovers or they would simply be friends who happened to have a brother and a sister who were married to each other.

One way was exciting, yet risky.

The other way was dull, but safe.

Clem could hardly wait.

The bachelorette party was taking place on Thursday, the day before the rehearsal. After many suggestions by the Bennelli sisters, Miranda decided she wanted to have her party at Vanessa's house in Sugar Land.

Valerie pouted. "I was looking forward to going to one of those male dancer places."

Clem rolled her eyes. She thought the whole idea of a bachelorette party was dumb, anyway, but she knew she was out of step with everyone else, so she kept her views to herself.

"I just want a quiet party with my girlfriends," Miranda insisted.

So Vanessa said she'd make a salad and provide the drinks and Clem and Valerie said they'd bring the pizza. They invited a half dozen of Miranda's girlfriends, including Annie and a couple of the Bennelli cousins as well as Mark's sister, Rebecca, and his sister-in-law Molly.

The night of the party, after everyone settled down to eat, Clem found herself sitting next to Rebecca. They exchanged pleasantries for a couple of minutes, then Rebecca said, "I saw your interview with Judge Pollock last week. I thought it was great."

Clem smiled happily. She was still basking in the glow of her first real success. "Thanks."

"Your job must be awfully interesting."

"It is right now, but it wasn't always." Because Rebecca's expression said she'd love to hear more, and because Clem didn't need much encouragement, anyway, she promptly launched into a recital of her troubles with Raymond.

"Funny how everyone probably thinks you've got it made because you work in such a glamorous profession, and you've got the same kinds of problems and frustrations that everybody else has," Rebecca said when Clem was finished.

"Boy, that's for sure. There is absolutely nothing glamorous about being a reporter. Yeah, the job can be interesting and challenging, but mainly it's just a lot of digging and persistence and plain old hard work."

"Yes, from what you've said, I can see that."

"Anyway, thanks to your brother Luke, I got that interview with the judge, and that made all the difference. Raymond *couldn't* ignore me after that."

Rebecca smiled. "It's typical of Luke to help out."

"Yes, I know how much he's done for your family since your dad died. It must be nice to know you have somebody like him that you can depend on." Clem was curious to know how Rebecca felt about Luke. Actually, she was curious to know about Luke, period.

"Well, yeah, I guess we are lucky to have him, but you know, Luke *loves* taking care of things." Rebecca took a bite of her pizza.

"Does he?"

"Sure. Just look at the way he jumped in to help you."

Clem nodded thoughtfully. What was Rebecca saying? That Luke liked to control things? He hadn't struck her that way. At least, not so far. But the thought was sobering. Clem had had enough of people trying to control her. God! Her mother and sisters were bad enough. She sure didn't need some man telling her what to do. "So what kind of work do you do for the company?" she asked

"I'm the office manager," Rebecca said.

"Do you like it?"

"Well...actually, no." She grimaced. "It bores me."

"I'd hate that," Clem said. "I can't imagine anything worse than being bored all the time."

"Exactly what I said to Luke last week."

"And what did he say?"

"He was surprised because I've never admitted how I felt before."

"So what are you going to do now that you have?"

"Well, if all goes the way I hope, I plan to go back to school." Rebecca set her plate down on the coffee table. Her gaze met Clem's again. "I've got my fingers crossed that Luke will go along with me."

"Why does it matter what *he* thinks?" Clem asked. "You're an adult. You can go back to school if you want to."

"Oh, I know. It's not that. Well, I mean, I *care* what Luke thinks, but, well, the thing is, I need money to go back to school full-time, the way I want to, so I've asked Luke to buy out my share of the company."

"Oh." Well, that put a different slant on things. Clem studied Rebecca. "Do you think he will?"

"I don't know. Right after we talked, he left for Austin. And so far this week he's been so busy, I hated to bug him. But I hope to get things settled tomorrow."

"You know, Rebecca," Clem observed, "even if your brother isn't able to buy you out, there's still no reason you can't find a job you like better."

"But without a degree, all I'm qualified to do is what I'm doing now. No, I really want to go back to school and finish my degree in advertising."

"Well, then, there are always student loans and student assistantships and that kind of thing. I had to get a loan to finish college. In fact, I just got the blasted thing paid off last year."

Rebecca nodded. "But it'd be so much easier if Luke will cooperate."

"I'm sure it would be, but I think you should do it no matter what." Clem was really warming to her subject. "I really believe people have to do what is right for them. No matter what anyone else says or what anyone else does. My family didn't want me to major in broadcast journalism. They thought I should study computers. But I knew what I wanted, so I did it. And for years they've been after me to get married, but that's not the life I want, so I pay no attention to them."

Rebecca mulled this over for a while, then grinned at Clem. "I like you, Clem. You're okay."

"The feeling is mutual," Clem said.

A while later Miranda announced that she and Mark had arranged to have the guests at the bachelor party meet the guests of the bachelorette party at Hound Dog, a popular karaoke club on Richmond. "That's why I wanted to start out here," she said.

"Oh, goody," Valerie exclaimed. "I've never been to a karaoke club."

"It sounds like fun," Annie agreed, "but I'm staying at my folks' house tonight, and I hate to get there too late, so I think I'll have to pass."

"What about you, Clem? You're coming, aren't you?" asked Vanessa.

Clem thought all that sing-along stuff was pretty silly. She was all set to beg off, on the grounds of how early she had to get up tomorrow, when the thought struck her that Luke might be there. "Yeah, what the heck," she said offhandedly. "Count me in."

The Hound Dog was housed in a low-slung, gray brick building with an unprepossessing exterior. It anchored a block-long strip center fronting on Richmond Avenue near the Loop. The only thing that set it apart from its neighbors was a large neon sign in the shape of a dog singing at a microphone.

Luke hadn't wanted to come. He'd been fighting exhaustion the entire evening, and after enduring several hours of what he considered to be a juvenile tradition of bedroom humor and backslapping at the bachelor party, he was ready to go home and hit the sack.

He'd been all set to say, "Count me out," when the thought struck him that Clem would probably be there. So here he was, entering the karaoke bar with the rest of the boisterous crew of Mark's male friends and family.

The interior of the club was dim and smoky, but the large stage was brightly lighted with two colored spots trained on a male singer backed by a big screen across which the lyrics to the current song were scrolling.

A soulful rendition of the Eagles' "New Kid in Town" was currently being performed. The singer was giving it his slightly off-key all. Luke wondered why anyone would want to get up in front of a bunch of strangers and make a fool of himself. Luke wouldn't get up there if his life depended on it, but different strokes for different folks, he guessed.

"Looks like we got here before the girls," Mark said, looking around. "Oh, no, there they are." He started waving, and Luke saw the group of women sitting at a long table off to the side. They waved back, and the men headed their way.

There was room at the table for some of the men and the others sat at flanking tables. Luke spied Clem at the very end of the table and walked over to her.

She looked up and smiled, and pleasure arrowed through him. Damn, but he was glad to see her! He pulled a chair over and sat down behind her.

She turned around. Her eyes were filled with warmth. "Hi," she said.

He grinned. "Hi." He wished they weren't surrounded by all these people because he wanted to kiss her. Badly.

"I wasn't sure you'd come to this place," she said.

"I almost didn't." He silently cursed the noisy club and all the people surrounding them. He didn't want to be talking to Clem in near shouts. He wanted to lean close and murmur in her ear. He wanted to tell her how glad he was to see her. And he wanted to get things straight between them. But he could do or say none of these things, so he contented himself with watching her.

During the next hour several members of their party got up to sing. At times Luke even found himself enjoying the show. Clem's sister Valerie, in particular, was very good, and she was fun to watch as she sang one of Bonnie Raitt's hits. And Luke laughed and catcalled along with the rest of them as his brother John, in a rare letting down of his hair, sang an energetic version of "Proud Mary."

But he stuck to his resolve not to get up there himself, even though his brothers urged him to join them in their rendition of the Oak Ridge Boys' "Elvira." Clem, however, did—after urging—join her sisters in their version of Three Dog Night's "Joy to the World."

Afterward, laughing, she declared, "I hate to break this up, but I'm a working girl."

"Oh, don't go yet," said one of the women.

"Gotta," Clem returned.

Luke looked at his watch. It was after eleven. He stood. "Me, too. I'll walk you outside."

She smiled her agreement.

He ignored the knowing looks from the others as he and Clem said their goodbyes.

The cool night air felt good as they exited the club. Without touching or talking they walked over to Clem's Jeep. Partly sheltered by the shadow of the car, Luke gently pulled Clem into his arms.

Without hesitation she lifted her face.

Still without speaking a word, he kissed her. When she twined her arms around him, he urged her closer, then backed her up against the Jeep and pressed against her.

He felt rather than heard the moan deep in her throat as his hands sought and found her breasts. Through the thin fabric of her blouse her heated skin bloomed under his touch, the nipples pushing against his seeking thumbs.

They kissed for a long time.

Finally, breath ragged and hearts thumping, they pulled apart. He leaned his forehead against hers and closed his eyes, fighting for control. His body throbbed. "I've been thinking about this for days," he said gruffly.

"Me, too," she whispered.

He drew back a little and looked deep into her eyes. "I think it's time we talked, don't you?"

"Yes. I was thinking the same thing."

The promise of things to come shimmered in the air between them. Luke wished he didn't have to say goodnight. At the moment what he wanted more than anything was to draw her close once more—to hold her and kiss her and touch her.

He wanted to take her home with him.

He wanted her to join him in his king-size bed, with the French doors open to the sounds of the fountain in the patio as they made slow, unhurried love to each other.

"I'd better go now," she said.

He sighed. "I know." He kissed the tip of her nose, then hugged her close for a long moment. "Do you want me to follow you home? Make sure you get there okay?"

She chuckled. "No, I'll be fine. I'm used to being on my own. Besides, I've got a car phone. And Mr. Rescue if I run into any trouble."

"I've got a car phone, too. Here, let me give you the number." Luke pulled his wallet out of his back pocket and withdrew one of his business cards. On the back he scribbled the number. "You can call me instead of Mr. Rescue if you need help."

Clem extracted a business card from her purse and wrote something on the back. She handed it to him, and there was laughter in her voice as she said, "Ditto!"

He kissed her one last time before helping her into the Jeep and waving goodbye.

He stood there until the red of her taillights was long gone. Then, with a deep breath, he turned and slowly walked to his car.

Chapter Seven

"*Another* new dress?" Alaina said in amusement. "There *must* be a new man in your life."

Clem could feel herself blushing. "My sister's getting married, and I have all these dress-up occasions," she offered lamely.

Alaina was obviously fighting a smile. "Oh, I understand perfectly."

"Listen, I don't have much time. I'm on my lunch break."

The teasing look disappeared, and Alaina was all business. "Okay, what is it you want?"

"I don't know...something, uh, you know...different."

"Sexy...different?"

Clem avoided Alaina's gaze. "Uh, yeah, sure. Why not?"

Twenty minutes later she walked out of Alaina's shop two hundred dollars poorer but with an absolutely beautiful dress in her hands and a keen edge of anticipation for the upcoming evening building in her belly.

She could hardly wait for the afternoon to end. The hours after lunch seemed to drag on forever, even though court was adjourned at three because Judge Pollock liked to get an early start on his weekend. Rumor had it that he took off for his cabin in Wimberley ten minutes after the courthouse emptied. Clem blessed him, and gratefully headed home.

By three thirty-five she was in the shower and using some of the scented bath gel her mother had given her at Christmas. The fragrant mixture of strawberry bath gel and steam permeated the bathroom.

By four she was blow-drying her long hair and trying to decide whether she wanted to French braid it the way she usually wore it or try something different. She decided she'd just twist it up in a loose chignon since the style was more suitable to the sophisticated dress she'd purchased.

By four-thirty she was dressed in her spiffy new royal blue dress with the crisscross straps front and back and the matching crisscross hemline that formed an inverted V and exposed a tantalizing glimpse of legs. She felt a deep sense of satisfaction as she looked at herself in the mirror.

Clem knew she was not beautiful—not by any stretch of anyone's imagination. She was too tall, too big boned, she had too many freckles and her look was too wholesome. Still, in this color—which *did* match her eyes, just as Alaina had said—and in this dress, with her hair styled this way, she felt beautiful, and maybe that was more important in the end.

At five minutes to five she'd finished her makeup, spritzed herself with perfume and fastened her new long, glittery earrings to her ears.

She was ready.

Promptly at five her doorbell rang.

A pleasurable tingle of butterflies erupted in her stomach as she took a deep breath before opening the door.

Oh, my, she thought, telling her heart to be still when she laid eyes on Luke, who looked drop-dead gorgeous in a navy pin-striped suit, dark tie and white shirt. Even though Clem usually eschewed the rigid confines of formal dressing, she had to admit there was something about a man in a suit....

He whistled softly as his gaze roamed over her. "You look terrific."

"Ditto," she said.

Then they both laughed, because it was exactly what she'd said the night before. And by the way he was looking at her, she knew he would have liked to pick right up where they'd left off then, too.

The memory of the kisses they'd shared and the passions they'd unearthed crackled in the air between them. Even the thought of those feelings caused an ache in Clem's nether regions, and her heart beat a little faster.

But duty called, in the form of the rehearsal and the dinner afterward, so Clem gave herself a mental shake and locked her apartment, then she and Luke headed for his car.

They talked casually as they drove to the church. Clem told Luke about the jury selection in the Spinosa case. When she'd finished, she said, "Now tell me about your trip to Austin. Exactly what kind of security job did you do there?"

"It was a security check—setting the company up to avert a security breach." He braked for a red light and turned on his left blinker. "What we do is, we go in, look over the crucial areas, see what kind of security is in place, then send someone in to test it and see if it works, and if it doesn't, we find out where the weak areas are."

"Someone to test it . . . like a spy?"

He smiled. "Sort of. Actually, more like a plain-clothes detective."

"So who does that for you?"

"We work with a private detective agency in Austin."

"That's interesting. So after you find the weak areas, what comes next?"

"Well, then we design a better system, one that will concentrate on plugging up those holes in the current system."

"What happened with this company? Did you find any security leaks?"

"Oh, we know there *are* some, but we're still in the preliminary stages of investigating, which consists of learning how things are done and who does them. It's a big company, with over a thousand employees, and lots of places where security can be breached. My brother Matthew was up there all this past week, and Paul will go back after the wedding, when we'll begin testing the potential problem areas." He muttered under his breath, "At least, I *hope* he's going back."

Clem thought the work sounded fascinating, kind of like a giant puzzle with missing pieces. She'd always liked that kind of work—digging her teeth into a problem and finding a solution. She wondered why Luke had said that about his brother Paul, but figured it was some kind of family thing, so she didn't pursue it.

They continued to talk comfortably, and more quickly than Clem would have believed possible, they'd arrived at the church.

St. Basil's was an old church close to her parents' home, the church where Clem had made her First Communion and her confirmation, the church where her parents had been married, as well as her twin sisters.

The church where Clem knew her mother still hoped Clem would be married, no matter how many times Clem said she had no intention of ever doing so.

But even though she knew she would never be a bride walking down the aisle, she had always had a soft spot in her heart for St. Basil's. It was small and beautiful, rich with stained glass and mellowed, dark wood and the scent of flowers—so different from the starkly modern churches in favor today.

She also had a soft spot in her heart for Father Ambrose, the pastor. He'd been the pastor there for as long as she could remember, and all the neighborhood children knew and loved him. As a kid Clem had spent a lot of time skating or playing basketball in the parking area to the back and side of the church, and Father Ambrose had always been there to cheer them on or to dispense antiseptic for bruised knees or hugs for bruised hearts.

Once inside the church, Luke smiled and squeezed her hand in farewell, then walked up to the front of the church to join Mark and his other brothers, while Clem stayed behind in the vestibule where Miranda and her sisters and mother were congregated.

"Is that another new dress, Clem?" her mother asked, raising her eyebrows.

"I've had it for a while," Clem replied. *It's not really a lie,* she told herself. After all, a while could mean months or weeks. *Or hours.*

"You look nice tonight, Mom," she added, to change the subject. Her mother *did* look nice in a softly flared red dress that complemented her gray hair.

"I see you came with Luke," her mother said, undeterred by Clem's attempt to sidetrack her.

"Yes, he offered to pick me up," Clem acknowledged as casually as she could manage.

"Oh, come on, Clem," Valerie said, "why can't you just admit you're dating him?" She gave Clem an arch look, and Vanessa giggled.

Clem hated that look. It was Valerie's Miss Texas look, the kind of look that always made Clem feel defensive.

"Yeah, Clem," echoed Vanessa, picking a piece of lint off the skirt of her lavender dress. "What are you afraid of? Why don't you just admit it?"

Miranda smiled happily.

Clem glared at them. "Because I knew if I did, this very thing would happen. You'd all make a big deal out of it. It's *not* a big deal. So can we please talk about something else?"

Her mother laughed softly. "Your prickles are showing, Clementine."

To Clem's intense relief, Father Ambrose entered the vestibule and said, "Hello Connie, Miranda—" his gaze moved around the circle "—Valerie, Vanessa and Clementine. How nice to see you all again. And don't you all look beautiful?"

As they were greeting him and exchanging pleasantries, the wedding coordinator arrived, and after that there was no more chance for conversation. Clem gratefully gave the coordinator her full attention. The woman quickly shepherded them all into line, motioning for Clem's father to join them, then began demonstrating the hesitation step they would take down the aisle.

She fussed over Miranda, telling her how to stand and what to do, then gave Clem her instructions. "Now remember," she said, "when you lift the veil, be careful not to mess up Miranda's hair."

"I know," Clem said.

For the next forty minutes they rehearsed and then Father Ambrose gave them a little pep talk. Clem liked the part where she and Luke linked arms and walked back down the aisle together, because that meant the whole thing would be over.

By seven o'clock they were all piling into cars and heading for Giovanni's, an elegant Italian restaurant on the Loop where the wedding party participants would meet the other members of the family who had been invited. Luke explained that he'd chosen Giovanni's not only because the food was superb but because Giovanni had been one of Luke's first customers when he'd gone into the business after his father's death. "Giovanni and my dad were friends," he explained, "and Giovanni was pulling for me to succeed."

Clem couldn't wait to get there. Her Bennelli grandparents had both passed away but her Clemente grandparents—for whom she'd been named—were both going to be attending the dinner. They had sold their Ohio home ten years ago and lived in Tucson now, and they'd flown in the day before and would stay for a week after the wedding.

She always loved seeing them. Her grandfather Clemente was a special favorite of hers, and she knew he felt the same way about her. She was looking forward to introducing him to Luke, too, because she thought they'd like each other. And wait'll Luke found out that it was her grandfather who had taught her to play pool!

When they entered the restaurant they were directed to the back room, which had been reserved for their party. There were already about a dozen people there, standing around talking and laughing. They threaded their way through the different groups, heading for the corner where Clem's grandparents stood talking with Luke's mother, Lucy.

Her grandparents looked wonderful, she thought. It was obvious the sun-filled climate of Tucson agreed with them. Her grandfather, in particular, looked as healthy as a man half his age. Joseph Clemente was eighty-six, erect of bearing, tanned and still showing evidence of the hard physical labor he'd done all of his life—now replaced by a daily regimen of eighteen holes of golf and an hour-long session with his weights. He still had a full head of hair, completely white, and his blue eyes, which Clem had inherited, still shone as brightly and sharply as they ever had.

Clem's gaze moved to her grandmother, who in so many ways was the opposite of her vigorous, physical husband. Doris Clemente was a tiny, frail-looking woman with a pale complexion and dark, wounded eyes. She had never completely recovered from the loss of one of her sons in Vietnam, and spent her days reading her Bible and writing in a journal. But despite her apparent lack of physical strength, she had a strong heart, and no serious health problems. Clem's mother had joked dozens of times how her mother would probably outlive her.

Clem, who was proud of her lack of sentimentality, felt misty-eyed as she looked at them. Memories of girlhood visits to their Ohio home came rushing back. She remembered how much fun it had been when Gramps had taken her and her brother Frank to the bowling alley on his bowling league night and let them gorge themselves on hot dogs and orange pop. She remembered her grandparents' huge garden filled with sweet corn and fat red tomatoes that they'd eaten with Grandma's crusty homemade bread. And she particularly remembered the Christmases they'd spent in Ohio—how she'd helped Gramps put the lights on the big blue spruce tree in the front yard and how she and Frank and Miranda always built a snowman Santa and how Gramps would take them all sledding in the park and ice-skating at the pond. All these happy memories tumbled through her mind in the moments before her grandfather turned her way.

"Clem!" he exclaimed, noticing her for the first time. His smile lit up his face, and he opened his arms to give her a hug. His strong arms enclosed her, and they hugged tightly, then kissed.

"Hi, Gramps," she said. "You look wonderful."

"And you look gorgeous. . . ." He turned to her grandmother. "Doesn't she, Doris?"

Clem's grandmother smiled softly. "Yes, she does."

Clem hugged her next, saying, "Grandma, I'm so glad you're here."

Then she turned to Luke's mother, a tall, spare, grayish blond woman who looked a lot like Luke. "Hello, Mrs. Taylor. It's good to see you again."

"Hello, Clem . . . Luke. How'd the rehearsal go?"

"Just fine," Luke answered. "Mark wasn't *too* nervous. He only stumbled once."

They all chuckled, then Clem said, "Grandpa, Grandma, this is Mark's brother, Luke Taylor. Luke, these are my grandparents—Joseph and Doris Clemente."

Luke and her grandfather shook hands, assessing each other in that way men have. "Very glad to meet you, sir," Luke said. Then he turned to her grandmother and took her hand, saying, "You sure have got a nice family, Mrs. Clemente."

Clem could see how his remark pleased her grandmother. Not for the first time, the thought crossed her mind that if she *had* been in the market for a husband, she probably couldn't find a more suitable candidate than Luke. He not only filled her criteria for a man, he filled her mother's. It was a scary thought, especially since there was a time when Clem would never have believed she and her mother would agree about anything.

"Tell me what's happening at the station," her grandfather said.

Clem never needed to be asked twice. She happily gave him a rundown of the past weeks' events.

"I'm so proud of you, my girl," he said, squeezing her waist and kissing her cheek.

Clem smiled at him, fighting against the almost bittersweet happiness that poured through her. She loved him so, and each time she saw him now, she was more aware of the passing of time and the inevitability that one of these reunions might be their last. "I love you, Gramps," she whispered, hugging him again.

"I love you, too, sweet pea," he answered gruffly, using his childhood pet name.

By now the rest of the wedding party had trickled in. A waiter circulated with glasses of wine and punch, and people gradually took their places at the various tables.

Two hours later Clem felt mellow and replete after a couple of glasses of wine and a perfectly wonderful dinner of fried calamari, stuffed mushrooms, Italian wedding soup, Caesar salad, angel hair pasta topped with shrimp and a luscious marinara sauce, and the pièce de résistance of mouthwatering Italian cream cake.

The waiters filled champagne flutes, and Luke, as the head of the groom's family and their host, stood to make the first toast.

"To my little brother," he began with a smile, "who's a braver man than I am..."

Everyone hooted.

Clem smiled. *Braver than me, too.*

"And to Miranda," Luke continued, "who's probably far too good for him..."

Mark grinned foolishly.

Miranda smiled.

"May they live a long and happy life together and may they hear the patter of many tiny feet."

The guests chorused, "Hear, hear," and everyone drank.

There were a couple more toasts and a few speeches, including a sentimental one from Clem's father and a sweetly loving one from Mark.

Afterward, the party began to break up. Clem walked around and said goodbye to everyone, then waited for Luke, who was settling the bill.

The butterflies she'd felt earlier in the evening returned as she remembered that she and Luke were going to talk about their relationship tonight.

She wondered what was going to happen between them. Would they become lovers? Or would they, after the wedding tomorrow, stop seeing each other entirely?

The last thought made her feel strangely bereft, a feeling she fought. She couldn't afford to let her emotions take over. She had to remain cool and in control.

Because no matter how much she liked him, if Luke wanted more than she was willing to give, she would *have* to call a halt to their relationship.

She would have no other choice.

Luke wondered what Clem was thinking. She'd been awfully quiet ever since they'd left Giovanni's. It wasn't like her to be so quiet.

Something must be wrong.

Since he believed in being direct, he said, "Something bothering you?"

"Hmm?" She gave herself a little shake, looked at him and smiled. "Oh...no, I, uh, was just thinking..."

"Want to share?"

Her eyes were luminous in the dark interior of the car. "Why don't we wait until we get to my place?" she said softly. "And then we'll talk."

Since they were only minutes away, Luke didn't push her. "All right." They drove the rest of the way to her apartment in silence.

Once they were inside her apartment, she kicked off her shoes and said, "Ahh, that's much better." She waved to a futon, which, next to a beanbag chair and a TV set, were the only substantial pieces of furniture in the room. "Sit. Make yourself comfortable. Do you want anything to drink? I haven't got much. Beer. Soda. Water."

Luke looked around, half amused, half disbelieving. Did she call this nearly empty apartment a home? "Uh, how about some coffee?"

"I can do coffee." She headed into the minuscule kitchen, visible over an open bar.

He loosened his tie, then removed it altogether. Oh, what the hell, he thought. He took off his jacket and unbuttoned the top button of his dress shirt. Now he felt much better, too.

Then he looked around curiously, noting the rest of the furnishings. She had two unpainted bar stools, and since he saw no table, he figured she ate her meals at the bar. Tacked to the walls were unframed travel posters of places like Rome and Paris and Stockholm and Cairo. Looked as if a yen for travel was something they had in common.

She also had a set of TV trays, two of which were opened and placed together in front of the futon and obviously functioned as a kind of coffee table. Next to the futon was a pole lamp, which she'd switched on when they'd entered the place. Lastly, there was a stack of magazines in the corner.

Luke wondered what this place said about Clem. He thought about how different his home was. It had taken the decorator months to get the place to his liking, and now it was a showplace.

He slowly walked over to the bar and leaned against it, watching her through the opening. She looked up as she poured water into a coffeemaker.

She smiled. "It'll be ready soon."

"I'm in no hurry." He continued watching as she removed some mugs from the cupboard, then opened the refrigerator, leaning over to peer inside. As she did, her dress tightened over her rear, delineating each curve and, much to his chagrin, causing Luke's hormones to leap to life.

"I'm afraid I haven't got any cream." She looked over her shoulder. "Milk okay?"

"I drink my coffee black." He told himself he was not some oversexed teenager, but boy, she certainly managed to make him feel like one. He wanted nothing more than to walk over there and caress that nicely rounded rump.

She straightened, a small plastic jug of milk in her hand. She removed the top and sniffed, then made a face. "Good thing, because this milk is bad, anyway."

Luke chuckled. "I'm beginning to think you don't spend a lot of time here."

She shrugged, dumping the milk down the drain. The coffeemaker gurgled, and the aroma of brewing coffee filled the air. "It's just a place to hang my hat. Temporary quarters."

"Temporary quarters? Are you moving?"

Her blue eyes met his. "Well, not right away, but you know...I think it's important not to have too many encumbrances. That way I can be ready to go at a moment's notice." When he didn't answer, she added, "You know, if I get a chance to go with the network."

He nodded. Of course. That explained the lack of furnishings, the obvious disregard for any kind of decorating.

He should have known.

If she made her apartment too homelike, it might be difficult to leave it. Well, her attitude made things easier, didn't it? She was apparently even less inclined than he was to make any kind of permanent commitment.

Still, no matter how things appeared, Luke had learned long ago not to assume anything. They needed to talk about this—get everything into the open and see where they stood. And now was as good a time as any.

He walked around to the doorway leading into the kitchen and leaned against it.

Only a few feet separated them.

Again her gaze met his. For a long moment the only sounds were the gurgle of the coffeemaker, the hum of the refrigerator and a faint sound of music from a neighboring apartment.

"Let's talk," he said, reaching for her hand.

She nodded, and he took her hand, intending to lead her into the living room and the futon where they could sit and have their discussion.

Instead, Luke found himself drawing her into his arms, the urge to kiss her, at least once, too strong to deny. She sighed as their lips met.

He tightened his arms around her, one hand splayed across her back, the other closing around her bottom—as he'd fantasized doing earlier—and pulling her close. He was already fully aroused, and he knew she could feel how much he wanted her.

It was a long, urgent, demanding kiss, and when he finally loosened his hold so that he could look into her eyes, they were both breathing fast and hard. "I want you, Clem. You know that, don't you?" His voice didn't sound like his own.

She wet her lips. "Yes," she whispered. "I want you, too."

He smiled. That was one of the things he liked best about her. Her directness. There was no subterfuge with Clem, and he didn't think there ever would be. "So what're we going to do about it?"

PLAY
ONE MILLION
BIG BUCK$
ONE MILLION
AND YOU COULD WIN THE
$1,000,000.00
PLUS JACKPOT!
YOUR PERSONAL GAME CARD INSIDE...
SILHOUETTE

IT'S FUN!

IT'S FREE!

BIG BUCK$

BIG BUCKS

S

HURRY!
This jackpot must be claimed!
Scratch here →

LUCKY CHARM GAME!

Claim 4 FREE books AND a FREE Mystery Gift!

YES! I have played my BIG BUCKS game card as instructed. Enter me in the MILLION DOLLAR Sweepstakes and also enter me for the Extra Bonus Prize. When winners are selected, tell me if I've won. If the Lucky Charm is scratched off, I will also receive everything revealed on the back of this page.

235 CIS AVZU
(U-SIL-SE-04/96)

NAME _____

ADDRESS _____ APT. ____

CITY _____ STATE ____ ZIP _____

NO PURCHASE OR OBLIGATION NECESSARY TO ENTER SWEEPSTAKES.   © 1993 HARLEQUIN ENTERPRISES LTD.

PRINTED IN U.S.A.

---

4 WAYS TO WIN BIG BUCKS!

1. Uncover 5 $ signs in a row….BINGO! You're eligible for a chance to win the $1,000,000.00 SWEEPSTAKES!

2. Uncover 5 $ signs in a row AND uncover $ signs in all 4 corners…BINGO! You're also eligible for a chance to win the $50,000.00 EXTRA BONUS PRIZE!

THE SILHOUETTE READER SERVICE™: HERE'S HOW IT WORKS

Chapter Eight

Fighting to control herself, knowing that her earlier admonition to remain calm and collected was the only way to go when her body was so determined to betray her, Clem took a deep breath and said, "C'mon. Let's go sit on the futon and talk."

In the few seconds it took them to walk to the futon and sit, she managed to calm herself a bit. She purposely sat facing him so that he would be forced to leave a few inches between them, because she still didn't trust herself to withstand this enormous physical pull between them.

And she needed a clear head!

Taking another deep breath, she said, "Before we can decide what we're going to do about this, uh, thing between us, there's something I have to tell you. And since I don't believe in beating around the bush, I'll come right out and say it. I *do* want you, but I have no interest in getting married or making a permanent commitment of any kind. If—" *Oh, God, it was hard to say this. But it had to be done!* "If," she repeated firmly, "that's what you're looking for, we should... probably call it quits right now."

Luke looked at her silently for so long, her heart slowly sank. She prepared herself to act as if it didn't matter when he said he preferred to call it quits.

After agonizingly slow seconds, he smiled. "Incredible. You stole the words right out of my mouth."

Surprise momentarily robbed her of any comeback other than a gaping, "Really?"

"Really."

"That... that's wonderful!" Although he'd said exactly what she was hoping to hear, she still didn't know what to say.

Apparently, neither did he.

Then he chuckled. "Do you feel as awkward as I do?"

She laughed, too, and a great sense of relief washed over her. "Yes. Why is that, do you think?"

He shrugged. "I don't know."

"Maybe it's because it's so unusual for a man and woman to talk about sex," she said thoughtfully.

His eyes twinkled. "You mean, as opposed to doing it?"

"Exactly."

"Well, I'm all for jumping right into bed and getting to the fun part," he teased, "but I want to be sure we both understand exactly what it is we're doing."

"Oh, I agree," she said fervently. "It's definitely best to get everything straight up front."

"Because we don't want any misunderstandings afterward."

"Absolutely not."

"So," he continued, "we agree we want to have a physical relationship, right?"

"Right, but that's it. No strings. No promises." She grinned. "No L words."

"And no M words," Luke added with a smile.

"Or even C words," Clem said.

"I *hate* C words," Luke agreed. "I'm committed to too many things as it is."

Clem took a deep breath. "What a relief! You can't imagine how glad I am that we agree. Wanna shake on it?" She extended her right hand.

They solemnly shook hands, then, a smile tugging at the corners of his mouth, Luke said, "How do you feel about S words?"

Clem grinned. "S words are fine. In fact, they're more than fine."

Laughing, he reached for her. "So what are we waiting for?"

Seconds later she was in his arms.

Clem decided she'd died and gone to heaven. Every fantasy she'd ever had about a man was in the process of being fulfilled.

She knew Luke wanted her. His urgency could be seen in his face, felt in the hardness of his body, heard in his voice.

But he didn't hurry.

He hauled her onto his lap, and they kissed for a long time. He touched her slowly, letting the momentum between them build, just the way Clem wanted him to. She touched him, too. First his chest, loosening several buttons of his shirt so that she could slide her hand inside and caress warm, firm skin and muscle. Then, later, more boldly, other places that beckoned. Clem loved hearing Luke's quick intake of breath as she stroked him, loved the answering urgency of his kiss, loved the hot lick of desire that suffused her.

After a while, touching through their clothing wasn't satisfying enough, and he began to unzip her dress, then stopped. "Shouldn't we go into the bedroom?" he said, his voice rough with passion.

"Well, uh..."

He drew back a little, and their gazes met. "What's the matter? Is something wrong?" He frowned. "You haven't changed your mind, have you?"

Clem shook her head, suddenly embarrassed. "No, I, uh, nothing like that...it's, uh, just that I don't have a bed in the bedroom," she finished in a rush.

An expression of disbelief scuttled across his face, quickly replaced by one of unbridled merriment. "So where do you sleep?"

Clem grimaced. "Here."

"Here? You mean...on the futon?"

She nodded. "When you open it up, it's actually very comfortable."

He laughed. "Clem, I can see it'll never be dull having a relationship with you. Well, come on, let's get it opened up."

Once they'd taken care of all the practical considerations—opened the futon and gotten the sheets on and made sure the blinds were closed and turned off the bright lights, and Luke had assured Clem he was prepared as far as protection went—the momentum that had built between them was mostly gone, but Clem decided that was okay, because Luke patiently began all over again.

Kissing.

Touching.

Murmuring.

It didn't take long for the desire between them to once more build to a fever pitch.

Only then did he go back to unzipping her dress, then whispered, "Let's take this off."

"Let's take all this off, too," she said, unbuttoning his shirt.

So they undressed each other, laughing softly as his hands fumbled with the clasp on her bra and her fingers refused to work fast enough removing his belt.

But finally they'd shed all encumbrances and they stood there in the glow of light from the kitchen, naked and filled with an almost unbearable anticipation.

"Clem," he said, his voice shaken and rough, his eyes raking her.

Clem felt just as shaken. Luke clothed was sexy and gorgeous. But Luke in the buff was beautiful. No other word described the flawless symmetry of his body, the perfect configuration of flesh, bones, sinew and muscle. Her eyes feasted on him, just as his feasted on her.

A deep yearning filled Clem, and even though she would have been the first to deny it, there was a part of her that strained toward Luke emotionally as well as physically.

On a quick intake of breath, he feathered his fingers across her breasts, then slowly down her body. She boldly did the same, filled with satisfaction as she saw how her touch affected him.

Shuddering, he drew her close and fitted himself to her in a way that caused her heart to begin a slow thudding in her chest.

"Clem, Clem," he muttered against her open mouth, "I want you so much."

She could feel how much, and there was an answering urgency in the liquid heat that unfurled within. "Yes," she moaned. "Yes."

They tumbled to the futon, and now their actions were hurried, because suddenly neither one could wait. They kissed hungrily, their tongues mating, their hearts pounding.

"Clem," he groaned.

And then he was thrusting into her, deeply, again and again, and she was lifting and clutching at his back, matching her movements to his until they'd found their rhythm.

All thought ceased. Now there was only this primal physical force, a force that would not be denied, a force that escalated, building momentum until it reached a shattering crescendo.

Afterward, they lay spent, arms wrapped around each other, hearts beginning to slow, breathing becoming more even and quiet. Clem snuggled deeper into Luke's embrace, and he kissed her softly, letting his tongue trace the contours of her mouth.

"The first time I saw you, I knew your mouth was made to be kissed," he said.

"You already told me that once," she teased.

"It bears repeating." He kissed her again, and she sighed. "Other things bear repeating, too." He rolled over onto his side, bringing her with him. His hand lazily stroked her.

"Umm," was all Clem could manage as he cupped her breast, then lowered his mouth to feather the nipple with his tongue.

He laughed softly. "But I don't think my back can take a repetition on this damned futon!"

And then Clem was laughing, too, and despite his complaints about "getting too old for this" and "at least you'd think she'd have a decent bed," the two of them did manage to repeat and even improve upon their first endeavor.

Afterward, as he dressed and Clem watched him, he said, "Will you come home with me after the wedding tomorrow night?"

Clem nodded, a warm glow of contentment enfolding her.

He sat on the edge of the futon, leaning over to kiss her lightly. "Bring clothes for Sunday. I've decided I'm going to take the entire weekend off and just have fun like the rest of the world. Anyway, we'll do something special, okay?"

"Okay."

He kissed her again. "Tonight was wonderful," he whispered. His green eyes glowed in the darkness. "*You* were wonderful."

"So were you."

He smiled. "I knew we'd be good together."

She started to say something flip, but said instead, "I have a feeling things are only going to get better."

When he left, she curled happily into the tangled sheets and fell asleep with the memory of his last kiss imprinted on her lips and the memory of his lovemaking imprinted on her body and the promise of the future imprinted on her brain.

Organ music filled St. Basil's, and the fragrance of Miranda's favorite camellias, along with roses and carnations, scented the air. The late-afternoon sunlight, rich with the jeweled tones of the stained-glass windows, shone down upon the guests, and throughout the lovely old church women dabbed at their eyes and men squirmed uncomfortably as unfamiliar emotions assailed them.

"Isn't she beautiful?" breathed Valerie, who was standing only inches from Clem's side. The two sisters watched as a radiant Miranda, on the arm of their father, walked up the long aisle toward the altar.

Clem nodded, fighting against the lump in her throat. She rarely got emotional, especially over something as clichéd as a wedding, but seeing her sister looking so luminous and happy stirred longforgotten memories of their childhood.

Clem and Miranda first learning to roller-skate, and how many skinned knees they'd both had.

Clem and Miranda pretending to be astronauts and Clem jumping off the top of the sliding board because she really thought she could fly.

Some stupid girl making Miranda cry when Miranda was in the third grade and Clem was in the sixth, and Clem punching the girl in the nose and making it bleed.

All these memories, like the fast-forward on a video, sped through Clem's mind, producing a jumble of emotions.

Of all her sisters, Clem felt closest to Miranda, and now, with Miranda on the threshold of a new life, Clem realized nothing would ever be the same between them. Her sister was moving on, leaving Clem and their past behind. She was happy for Miranda, because she knew this was what Miranda wanted, but that happiness was bittersweet and tinged with a sense of loss.

Clem looked at her father—his proud expression and glowing eyes as he glanced down at his daughter. Her gaze moved next to her mother, who sat smiling and misty-eyed in the second row, then to her grandparents. The lump got bigger as Clem's grandfather's eyes met hers, and he smiled at her.

She swallowed, willing herself not to cry. She looked away, to the other side of the church, as she fought to get her emotions under control.

And then her gaze met Luke's.

The memories of her childhood faded away, to be replaced by new memories of last night. She smiled. Her vague sense of loss and unhappiness was supplanted by a delicious tingle of excitement and a flurry of anticipation for all the days and nights ahead of her.

Luke looked breathtakingly handsome in his black tux, she thought as her eyes drank him in. The groomsmen and ushers were all wearing burgundy cummerbunds and tiny pink rosebuds in their breast pockets to complement the bridesmaids' mauve taffeta dresses and bouquets of pink and white roses and baby's breath.

If anyone had told Clem she'd actually enjoy wearing a pink taffeta dress, she'd have laughed in their face, and yet she had to admit the dress made her feel feminine and almost beautiful.

The dress really was lovely—styled along simple princess lines with a low, square neckline, close-fitting short sleeves and torso, and a gently flaring skirt that ended midcalf. Paired with satin pumps in the same color, the ensemble was classically elegant.

Each of the bridesmaids had tiny pink roses twined in their hair, and Miranda had gifted her sisters with a single strand of pearls to wear today.

Clem could see by the expression on Luke's face that he thought she looked beautiful, too.

Just then Miranda and their father reached the altar where Father Ambrose stood waiting, an open prayer book in his hands.

A beaming Mark, his eyes for Miranda alone, joined his bride-to-be, and the two turned to face the priest. A hush fell over the assembled guests.

"Dearly beloved," Father Ambrose intoned. "We are gathered together here in the sight of God..."

Clem listened as the familiar words were spoken. Throughout, she attended to her duties, and the ceremony proceeded smoothly.

And then it was over and Clem slipped her hand under Luke's arm. He smiled down at her as they walked down the aisle to the accompaniment of the familiar recessional played with enthusiasm by one of Clem's cousins, who was serving as the organist.

When they reached the vestibule, there were only a few seconds for Luke to squeeze her hand and say warmly, "Save me a dance at the reception," before releasing her to join the receiving line.

After greeting all the wedding guests, the wedding party and families piled into cars for the short drive to the country club where the reception was being held. Clem rode with Luke, but there was no chance for private conversation between them because they were joined by Valerie and her husband, Jeff.

Instead, the four of them talked about how nice the ceremony had been and how beautiful Miranda looked and how glad they were things had gone off without a hitch.

"Dad's getting to be an old hand at this, isn't he?" Valerie said to Clem.

"Yeah, he is."

"Well, he's almost finished with giving away daughters," Valerie added. "Now there's only you left, Clem."

"No, he's finished," Clem said, shooting Valerie a dirty look. When she turned around, Luke's amused eyes met hers and he winked.

A little later, when he braked for a red light, he reached over and squeezed her hand as he had earlier and smiled at her. A pleasurable tingle slid through Clem.

Oh, she liked this man!

And thank goodness he had the same ideas about life that she did. But she was still irritated with Valerie for saying something so obvious in front of Luke. What if he'd been the kind of guy to get turned off by broad hints like that? Clem decided she'd have a word or two with Valerie the first chance she got.

Once they reached the reception, there were more duties—the obligatory greeting of guests, handling of gifts and helping out where she was needed—but finally, as the small combo struck up the first dance number, Clem was free to enjoy herself.

She stood talking with Annie and Bradley and waited for Luke to join her. Out of the corner of her eye she could see him gradually making his way in her direction.

"I see you looking at Luke," Annie teased, leaning over to whisper in Clem's ear.

"I am not!"

Annie just smiled knowingly. "Deny it all you want, but I know what I see. Are you two an item now?"

"Did I tell you how much I like your outfit?" Clem countered just as if Annie hadn't asked her a question. Annie *did* look smashing in a gorgeous black raw-silk suit paired with a black sequined evening hat with a frothy veil that set off her strawberry blond hair to perfection.

"Quit trying to change the subject," Annie replied, eyes twinkling.

"I think I'll go get some champagne," Bradley interjected. "You two want some?"

Clem and Annie both nodded their agreement, and Bradley walked off.

"I'm waiting," Annie said.

Clem sighed. "Oh, all right. Yes, we're dating. But that's it! We're not *an item,* as you put it."

Annie smiled happily. "Oh, Clem, I'm so *happy* for you! He's such a dreamboat!"

Clem rolled her eyes. Honestly! Annie was so ridiculously romantic. Dreamboat! Who called anyone a dreamboat nowadays? "You've been watching too many old Cary Grant movies," she said crossly.

"Well, so what? Besides, he *is* a dreamboat," Annie insisted. She squeezed Clem's waist. "And speaking of dreamboats, here he comes."

Clem wanted to be cool. She didn't want Annie or Luke or anyone, for that matter, to suspect how profoundly Luke affected her. But no matter how she tried, she couldn't stop the fluttering in her stomach or the increased tempo of her heartbeat as he approached.

She did manage to smile casually, as if he were just an ordinary acquaintance.

He smiled back. "How'd I get so lucky?" he asked. "The two most beautiful women in the room, and I've got them all to myself."

Clem rolled her eyes. "Oh, please, I look like a big pink Easter bunny in this getup!"

"You do not!" Annie said. "Does she, Luke?"

"She most certainly does not." Then, obviously fighting a grin and losing, he added, "She looks more like a big cotton candy."

"Big cotton candy!" Clem turned to give him a mock punch.

He deflected the punch, then put his hand around her waist and bent over to whisper in her ear, "Good enough to eat."

Clem knew she was blushing and she could have strangled him. Jeez! Now Annie was sure to think things were serious between her and Luke.

Sure enough, Annie's eyes were shining. Clem knew Annie was probably already planning the wedding. Oh, brother, just what Clem needed!

Just then Bradley returned with the champagne, and the four of them talked for a few minutes. A song ended and a new one began.

"Miss Bennelli," Luke said, bowing formally, "may I have the pleasure of this dance?"

Clem put down her glass of champagne and walked into Luke's arms. He held her very close as they slow danced to the strains of the Carpenters' "We've Only Just Begun," which had always been one of Clem's favorite songs. She restrained herself from humming along, since she'd been told more times than she could count that she couldn't carry a tune.

The first time around the floor they didn't talk, but then, his mouth close to her ear, he murmured, "I couldn't get to sleep last night."

Clem's heart skipped. "Oh?"

"I kept thinking about you."

Clem swallowed.

Before she could think of an appropriate answer, he asked, "Did you think about me?"

"Nope. Slept like a baby."

He laughed, pulling back to look at her face. "You're not a good liar, Clem, did you know that?"

She pretended indignation. "What makes you think I'm lying?"

"Oh, nothing much . . . just that you can't look me directly in the eyes . . . and you're blushing."

"I am not!" she said hotly, but she knew she was.

In answer, he pulled her even closer and nuzzled his mouth against her ear, causing a deliciously shivery sensation all the way down to her toes. "I love it when you blush," he whispered. When she didn't answer, he chuckled. "I can't wait to get you in my bed tonight." His breath feathered her ear. "I've been thinking about it all day long."

If Clem had been a cat, she'd have purred. The most erotic images filled her mind, and liquid heat gushed through her veins. "I—I really think we should talk about something else," she said breathlessly.

"Do you?" His voice was low, intimate and oh, so sexy.

It was getting more difficult to breathe all the time. "Uh-huh."

"And why is that?"

"Because people are watching us."

"Since when do you care what people think?" he observed with infuriating male logic.

Clem took a deep breath and told herself to get a grip and quit acting like a stupid kid. "I don't, not really," she said rather primly, "but I'd just like to avoid speculation about our relationship, because, knowing my family, it won't stop there. They'll start hounding me, and I don't need that."

She pulled back a little. "Remember our agreement? No strings? None of those serious words? We're just in this to have fun."

He grinned, eyes dancing with merriment. "I *am* having fun. Teasing you is loads of fun."

"Come on, Luke. Why get everyone thinking our relationship is serious when we know it isn't? Won't that just complicate our lives?"

"You've got a point, I guess," he conceded.

"Well, don't you think we should practice a little discretion, then?"

He nodded solemnly. "Okay, okay. I promise to be the soul of discretion in public." But his eyes were still dancing, and the corners of his mouth twitched.

"And stop laughing at me!" she said.

In answer, he just laughed harder, and twirled her around the room, which made her laugh, too. When the song finished he walked with her back to where she'd left her champagne, but a zealous waiter had already removed the glass.

"Want more?" he asked.

"Not right now. I'm too warm from all that exertion." She fanned herself to illustrate her point.

He grinned. "That's not why *I'm* warm."

If Clem had had something in her hand, she would have thrown it at him as he walked away, still laughing.

Chapter Nine

Luke was having the time of his life. He couldn't remember the last time he'd so thoroughly relaxed and enjoyed himself.

Clem was good for him, he decided. Teasing her, sparring with her, dancing with her, flirting with her, trying to make her blush—all were having the effect of the most powerful aphrodisiac.

He remembered reading somewhere that anticipation was half the fun of anything, and that was certainly proving to be true tonight. As much as he could hardly wait to get her home, in his bed, just as he'd suggested earlier in the evening, he was certainly enjoying thinking about it. And the more he thought about it, the more eager he became.

Eager! Turned on is more like it....

He laughed to himself. He hadn't been so turned on by a woman in years. Maybe he'd *never* been this turned on.

Clementine Bennelli, you just wait, he promised silently as he watched her dancing with one of her brothers-in-law. *Tonight I plan to make your toes curl!*

He decided he enjoyed watching her almost as much as dancing with her himself. Clem was fun to watch. She never did anything halfway—he'd already learned that—and dancing was no exception.

Right now the band was playing Chubby Checker's "Twist and Shout," and Clem and her brother-in-law were doing a mean version of the dance. Clem was laughing, and her eyes were shining, and she was clearly having a ball.

As Luke watched, Clem and Mark—who was dancing with Miranda—bumped into each other, and that made her laugh even harder. Just then her gaze met his, and she waved and grinned. Luke waved back.

"Is it true what I hear?"

Luke turned to see his brother John standing next to him. "That depends. What have you heard?"

John inclined his head in Clem's direction. "That you're dating her—Miranda's sister Clem."

"Who told you that?" Luke hedged.

John smiled. "You should know it's impossible to keep a secret in our family."

Luke knew Clem wanted to downplay their involvement, and in this he concurred. He had no wish to be quizzed about Clem, nor did he want to be the target of well-meaning, if misdirected, hints about marriage or anything else. He turned to meet John's speculative gaze. "Look—this is no big deal. I've dated lots of women."

"All right," John said. "I get the hint. I'll mind my own business."

The brothers stood there quietly for a moment, then Luke asked, "How're *you* doing tonight?"

John shrugged. "I'm okay."

Luke studied his younger brother. The entire family had been worried about him for the past year—ever since Cathy, his wife of eleven years, had died of leukemia, leaving John with two young children to raise, as well as a grief-stricken heart. They'd all known today would be tough on him because he was bound to be haunted by memories of other weddings, his own included.

But he did seem to be doing all right. Luke hesitated a moment—the Taylors were not naturally a demonstrative family like the Bennellis—then squeezed his brother's shoulder in sympathy.

"You know," John said after a while, "I've learned a lot in the past year." He stared at the dancers. "I've learned you shouldn't sweat the small stuff. That you should be happy with what you have and enjoy each day and tell the people you love how much they mean to you."

Luke saw John blink, then swallow, and knew his brother was fighting to control his emotions. Luke felt his own eyes stinging and said gruffly, "You have no reason to feel regret. Cathy knew you loved her."

"I know, but I just wish I'd told her more often." He grimaced. "The trouble is, I didn't realize how much I loved her until she was gone. And then . . ." He hesitated. "And then I realized I wasn't complete without her."

Silence fell between them again. Luke wondered what it would be like to feel that way about a woman. He didn't think he ever wanted to. It would give another person too much power over him.

His gaze searched out Clem again. Thank God she felt the same way he did. They were taking what they wanted from their relationship, and when it was over, they'd say goodbye like two sensible, rational human beings, and that would be that.

"Luke?"

"Uh, yeah?" Luke responded, shaking the thoughts of Clem free.

"Rebecca told me about asking you to buy her out."

Luke sighed. He and Rebecca still hadn't settled anything. She'd wanted to talk to him about her request on Friday, but he'd put her off, saying Monday was a better day for the discussion.

"Are you going to do it?" asked John.

"I don't know." Even though John was his brother, Luke didn't feel like telling him that coming up with the money to buy out Rebecca would mean he'd have to either cash in some of his investments or sell his house, neither of which he really wanted to do. Both the investments and the equity in his house were earmarked for the time when he would be free to quit the company and pursue his own goals.

"You know," John said slowly, "there's something I've been meaning to talk to you about, too."

Luke turned his head sharply. "Don't tell me *you* want to be bought out, too!"

"No, no, nothing like that! I, uh, wanted to talk to you about quitting fieldwork altogether. I want to be free to spend more time with my kids."

Luke groaned inwardly, but he forced himself to keep his voice nonaccusatory. "Can we discuss this at the office next week? I don't want to think about work or the company right now."

"Oh, yeah, sure," John said hurriedly. "I didn't mean to bring it up now. It's just that we were talking about Rebecca . . ." His voice trailed off.

"It's okay. I understand." He *did* understand where John was coming from, but Luke was tired of being the one who was supposed to make everything work out all right for everyone else, especially since his own life was crowded with unfulfilled dreams and ambitions that seemed to have less and less chance of coming to fruition. He guessed what he was really sick of were the demands of his family.

Thank God for Clem, he thought. At least with her he could forget everything. At least she placed no demands on him, except ones he was happy to fulfill.

He resolutely closed his mind to his problems with his family. This weekend he would do nothing but enjoy being with Clem.

When "Twist and Shout" was over, Clem looked around for Luke. The last time she'd seen him, he'd been standing near the bar talking to his brother John.

He was no longer there.

She wiped her forehead with a tissue, then decided she'd better head for the ladies' room where she could better repair the damage to her hair and makeup. When she entered, the room was empty except for two women, both unknown to her. One was a petite brunette in a short black dress. She stood putting on fresh lipstick in front of the mirror. The other woman was tall and slender and had silvery blond hair and the most impressive breasts Clem had ever seen outside of the movies. They were shown to advantage in a low-cut red dress. The blonde was combing her hair.

The women glanced at Clem and smiled. Clem smiled back. She moved to a vacant sink and turned on the cold water so she could cool off her face.

"So," said the brunette, "have you talked to Luke yet?"

Clem's ears perked up. Luke?

"No," the blonde said. "Not yet." She tugged at her cleavage and smiled. "But I will." She took a deep breath and arched her back. "What do you think?"

The brunette grinned. "If that dress doesn't do it, nothing will."

The blonde smiled in satisfaction. "That's what I thought." A moment later the two of them left the room.

Clem hurriedly finished her own grooming repair work and hightailed it out of the ladies' room so she could see if the Luke they'd been talking about was her Luke. *Whoa! Wait a minute! Luke isn't your Luke. Get that thought out of your mind!*

Okay, okay, fine, she answered herself, *but I have a right to be curious, don't I?*

She slowly made her way through the crowd, eyes trained for the blonde or for Luke. Within minutes she spied them.

Together.

The blonde was hanging on his arm, and he was grinning down at her. *And* he was staring at those spectacular breasts of hers, Clem noticed. In fact, he couldn't seem to tear his eyes away from them.

Clem clenched her fists as a sharp, bright shaft of jealousy knifed her. She stared at them, her heart beating too fast, her face suddenly too hot. She had an insane urge to tromp over there and yank the blonde away from him. She wanted to slap her stupid face. Actually, she wanted to slap *his* stupid face!

You don't have any claims on Luke. Remember what you reminded him of earlier? No L words? No C words?

Clem gritted her teeth.

You have no right to be jealous or possessive or anything else. If Luke wants to ogle that blonde, he has every right to ogle her.

Yes, but...

No yes, buts. You can't have it both ways.

Clem sighed.

"I see you sending daggers Luke's way," Miranda observed, walking up next to her in a swish of satin.

"I am not! I was just watching Luke and that woman dance...because they're good."

Miranda chuckled. "Oh, I understand...."

"Good."

Miranda leaned closer. "Don't worry. Mark told me that woman has been trying to get her hooks into Luke for years, and he's not interested."

"I wasn't worrying," Clem said.

"Well, just in case you were, I thought I'd reassure you." Miranda's blue eyes sparkled.

"I don't need reassuring," Clem insisted. "Uh, who is she?"

Miranda laughed. "Her name is Toni Chapman, and she's the widow of a cousin of Mark's and Luke's. Evidently she always had an eye for Luke—even when she was married—and she's been chasing after him ever since her husband died."

Clem nodded and forced herself to stop looking at them. She decided she was hungry and once more headed for the buffet table, where she loaded a plate with shrimp, miniature egg rolls, little sandwiches and tiny shish kebabs, adding a deviled egg and several olives for good measure.

She walked over to the tables and found a seat at a table with Luke's sister, Rebecca, and a bunch of people she didn't know. "Mind if I join you?" she asked.

"No, of course not," they chorused.

She sat down and began eating. Out of the corner of her eye she could still see the red dress and silvery blond hair of Toni Chapman. She was still hanging on Luke's arm, and he was still laughing. As she watched, they once more headed for the dance floor, where Luke took the woman into his arms and they began to dance. They were smiling at each other and dancing very close together.

Clem stuffed an egg roll into her mouth and chewed furiously.

"I've been watching your coverage of the Spinosa trial," a man sitting next to Rebecca said. He grinned at her. He had an open, friendly face and reminded Clem of a giant teddy bear. "You're doing a great job."

"Thanks," she replied around the mouthful of food.

"I'll bet there's lots of stuff you can't report on the air," he continued.

Clem tried to concentrate on what the man was saying and to stop watching Luke and Toni Chapman. She knew she was being ridiculous. She knew she had no right to feel this way. But she was seething with jealousy. She forced herself to answer the teddy bear and smile at him. And when she was tempted to search out Luke and the blonde, she ate more food instead.

So a few minutes later, as the combo took a break and the dancers drifted off the floor, she was unprepared for Luke's hand on her shoulder. She jumped when he leaned down and said, "I've been looking for you."

Her fairy godmother was probably looking after her, Clem decided later. Because she was surrounded by people within earshot, she couldn't say something sarcastic like, "Oh, yeah, I saw what you were looking for, and it sure wasn't me!" and make a complete fool of herself.

That was a close call, Bennelli, she told herself as she and Luke danced together later. She knew that not only would she have felt like an utter idiot if she'd shown Luke how jealous she was, but she'd have scared him off fast. So when he asked her if she was having fun, she answered lightly, "I'm having a great time!"

He smiled, pulling her closer into his embrace. "And just wait until I get you alone.... "

* * *

Clem knew Luke's house would be nice, but she hadn't been prepared for just *how* nice, or how much she'd love it.

It was just the sort of house she would have enjoyed living in—if she'd *wanted* that kind of encumbrance, she amended. It was spacious and cool looking, perfect for the muggy Houston climate. All the walls were painted white, and there were white ceiling fans in every room. The floors were beautiful Mexican tiles in a warm terra-cotta shade. Dark beams gave the high ceilings a rustic touch, and the enormous stone fireplace dividing the living room from the dining room was open on either side.

Luke's furniture was all deep-cushioned in colors of oatmeal and ochre and sand with accent colors of navy and tangerine. In his dining room was a rectangular dining table of heavy glass supported by dark oak pedestals. The other wooden pieces were all gleaming dark wood—either old and restored or designed to look old and restored. In either case, they worked beautifully to set the tone of the house. Dotted around the rooms were sculptures and vases reflecting the Southwest and its varied cultures, with lots of beaten brass and old, gleaming silver. There were dozens of floor-to-ceiling windows, and Clem knew that during the day the house would be flooded with sunlight.

But the most intriguing aspect of the house was the array of pictures. Everywhere Clem looked was evidence of Luke's interest in photography. Framed photographs, both black-and-white and color, hung everywhere. They showed children at play, old people at rest, couples with linked arms, men and women of all walks of life in every imaginable situation.

Included among them were several he'd taken at the picnic three weeks earlier. Two of the photographs were of her—one where she was jumping up and down about something her team had done, the other of her sliding into home plate. All of the photographs had one element in common: they were fascinating studies of character and emotion.

"These are great," Clem said softly. She was impressed. His work was wonderful. Much better than she'd imagined. In fact, she couldn't understand why anyone as talented as Luke hadn't tried to do something with his talent—responsibilities or not. Especially since he claimed to want to make photography the focus of his life. Once more she wondered what was keeping him from doing so.

He smiled. "You make a good subject."

"It's more than that, Luke. You're really good. I'm no expert, of course, but I think much of this work is brilliant."

"Thanks."

Clem would have liked to pursue the subject, but he was already leading the way into the kitchen. She made a mental note to reopen the subject of his ambitions in the near future.

The kitchen was big and airy, done in tones of peach to harmonize with the terra-cotta floor tiles, and there were copper pots and red clay flowerpots and tons of green plants everywhere. The room looked like something out of *Better Homes and Gardens*. Clem thought about her own kitchen and chuckled.

Luke slowly showed her through the remainder of the house. In addition to the main living areas, he had a small bookcase-lined office, a good-size darkroom and three bedrooms. The entire house was built in a U shape around a central patio, and one of the wings held the master bedroom suite, which Luke showed her last. It opened directly into the patio via long French doors.

Clem coveted the patio immediately. She could just see herself there in the evenings, relaxing with a cold drink and her notes for the following day. The soothing sound of a fountain gurgled in its center, and in the illumination cast by dozens of tiny lights ringing the perimeter of the area, Clem could see the masses of flowers and shrubs, including a couple of huge crepe myrtle that were tall enough to qualify as trees. There were even wind chimes, tinkling softly in the breeze.

Clem sighed. Perfection.

And Luke's bedroom! *Wow,* she thought, using her favorite exclamation. It was an enormous room dominated by a huge four-poster bed. The furniture was massive and dark, just like the pieces in the living room and dining room, but the whiteness of the walls and the openness to the outdoors kept the room from any sense of gloom. Unlike the main living areas, this room was carpeted in plush gray, and the accent colors in the room, reflected in the upholstery of two armchairs that graced one corner and a quilt folded over an antique chest, were turquoise and jade.

"Do you like it?" Luke asked. "Even though I bought the house as an investment, I wanted it to be a place that I enjoyed coming home to." He was removing his cummerbund and bow tie, smiling as he watched her reaction. "I had a decorator do the whole thing."

"Like it? I love it," Clem breathed. "It's wonderful. The whole house is wonderful." For the first time in her life Clem envied someone their possessions, and it was a disturbing feeling.

Not that she'd never been envious. Certainly she had. She'd been envious of other reporters many times, coveting their assignments and accomplishments. When she'd been younger she'd even been envious of other women and the way they looked.

And just tonight—she blushed even thinking about her ridiculous pangs of jealousy over that Chapman woman. But she'd never before coveted *things*.

Until now.

She looked at Luke. He stopped in the middle of removing his shoes and tilted his head quizzically.

"What?"

She shook her head. "Nothing." She smiled. "I'm impressed, that's all."

"Are you?" He finished kicking off his shoes, then walked over to her, drawing her into his arms. He tilted her chin up and searched her eyes for a long moment. When he spoke again, his voice was teasing. "Shall we get started on other things that might impress you even more?"

She laughed. "Aren't you *ever* serious?"

"I spend most of my life being serious. That's why I like being with you." He kissed her softly, slowly, then with the tip of his tongue traced the contours of her lips. Then he dropped his head and kissed the hollow of her throat, moving his warm mouth down, down.

His tongue dipped into the valley between her breasts. "With you," he whispered, "I can just enjoy myself."

Clem's breath caught and her bones felt as if they might melt if he kept it up.

"Do you like that?"

"Umm . . ." was all she could manage.

"I didn't think the reception would ever be over." His lips trailed up again, nuzzling against the corner of her mouth. He took her hand and placed it against him. "Feel that? I want you, Clem. I want to make love to you," he whispered.

Clem's heart skidded with excitement. There was an answering urgency in her own body, the same heat and desire that emanated from his.

"Do you want me to?" he continued.

"Yes," she whispered. "Oh, yes."

He released her slowly. "Good." They looked at each other for a long moment, then he led her to the bed. "Sit here for a minute," he said. "There's something I have to do first. . . ."

Clem couldn't imagine what Luke was doing. She could hear him in the next room, which she assumed was the bathroom, but he'd shut the door. She was tempted to go over and open it, but she didn't.

Instead, she removed all the flowers from her hair and took off her shoes and jewelry. She was debating over removing her dress when Luke opened the door and beckoned to her. The sound of running water came from behind him.

Clem gasped as she entered the huge bathroom. Dominating the center of the room was an enormous elevated oval tub that was circled by three shallow marble steps. Steaming water gushed into the tub via Jacuzzi jets, and Luke must have used some kind of bubble bath, because bubbles were erupting everywhere.

But that wasn't what drew Clem's attention. Her eyes widened as she saw that on the marble steps leading to the tub Luke had placed dozens of candleholders of every size, shape and description, and they were all filled with lighted candles. She slowly looked around. Shadows danced across the walls and ceiling, which contained a large skylight centered right over the tub. The far wall had a floor-to-ceiling paned window. Tiny outdoor lights showed a completely private atrium area with a brick wall in the background.

"Well?" Luke asked.

"I—I'm speechless," Clem said.

Luke grinned. "Good. It isn't speech I want from you, anyway. Now come here, woman...." He reached for her.

As their lips met in a heated kiss, Clem decided there was a lot to be said for silence.

"Wake up, sleepyhead."

Clem groaned and burrowed deeper into the pillow.

"Come on, wake up."

She groaned again. She wanted the voice to go away. And then she felt warm lips nuzzling her back, felt the sheet that was covering her being pulled lower, felt a breeze on her naked backside....

Naked backside! Wait a minute!

She sat up abruptly, nearly conking Luke on the head. Memories of the previous night came flooding back, and she grabbed for the sheet, covering her exposed breasts with one hand while she rubbed her eyes and tried to come fully awake with the other.

A gorgeously naked Luke sat next to her on the bed. He seemed amused by her show of modesty. "You sure look cute in the morning," he drawled.

Clem wished she had something to throw at him. She hated people who were cheerful in the morning. "What're you grinning about?" she grumbled.

"Oh, so we're cranky in the mornings, are we?"

"Don't talk about me in the plural." Damn, she needed coffee. Strong coffee. "What time is it, anyway?"

"Long past time to get moving." He tugged at the sheet. "Come on, let's go. Up and at 'em."

"Tell you what. I'll get up and at 'em, as you put it, if you'll get me a cup of coffee."

"Your wish is my command." Not acting in the least embarrassed by his lack of clothing, he winked and walked out of the bedroom. She could hear him whistling as he made his way to the kitchen.

Clem looked at the bedside clock. "Oh, God." It read 8:30. Why were they getting up so early? Hadn't it been about three-thirty before they'd ever gotten to sleep last night?

When Luke returned a few minutes later he held two mugs of steaming coffee in his hands. He handed her one, then stood sipping and looking down at her as she took her first, wonderful mouthful. After a second swallow she said crossly, "Why don't you put on some clothes?"

He chuckled. "Are you *always* this cranky in the morning?"

"Yes. Wanna make something of it?"

"I wouldn't dream of it." His eyes twinkled above the rim of the cup. "Does my nakedness bother you?"

"It's a little disconcerting, yes."

He grinned. "Does it make you hot for my body?"

"No, it doesn't," she said primly.

He laughed. "Liar." Then he walked over to the bed and carefully placed his mug on the bedside table. Next he reached for hers and put it beside his. Then he climbed back into bed, where he proceeded to take her into his arms and kiss her until she was dizzy.

"*Now* are you hot for my body?" he whispered, his fingers seeking and finding a place that made her moan. "Are you?"

"Yes, yes, yes!" she said.

For a long time after that they didn't talk.

Chapter Ten

"So what do you have planned for the day?" Clem asked much later, after they'd finally left Luke's bed, had a leisurely breakfast of pancakes and bacon, and gotten dressed.

Luke smiled down at her. She sat Indian-fashion in a large wicker chair and looked sexy as all get-out in her white shorts and royal blue T-shirt and cute little white sneakers. "I thought we'd go to the zoo."

"The zoo! You've got to be kidding." She gave him a quizzical smile. "You *are* kidding, aren't you?"

"Nope."

"But why the zoo?"

"Because I haven't been to the zoo since I was a kid, and it just sounds like fun. Remember? You and I are supposed to be having fun."

"Hey, I *always* have fun."

She lazily unfolded herself from the chair, stood and stretched. The motion caused her T-shirt to tighten over her breasts, but she seemed completely unaware of the revealing stance. There was no embarrassed dropping of her arms, nor was there any kind of knowing look in her guileless blue eyes.

Luke gave himself a little mental shake. "Well, humor me, okay? If you'll go to the zoo with me this morning, I'll do whatever you want to do this afternoon."

"Whatever I want to do, huh?" Her eyes sparkled with teasing humor. "Now *that* could be interesting." She made a show of serious thinking, then said, "What if I want to tie you up and make you my prisoner and force you to do unspeakable things?"

"If that's what you have in mind, why wait until this afternoon?" Laughing, he held out his hands, wrists together. "Do with me what you will, oh, master...."

She gave him a playful punch. "Jeez, you men! I should have known all I had to do was mention something kinky, and you'd be all hot to trot!"

They had just made love not two hours earlier, but looking at her now—all bright-eyed and bushy-tailed—Luke wanted to haul her back into his arms and kiss her senseless. It was unbelievable. Every caveman juice in his body was stirring. Yes, she was definitely good for him. "Hey, you're the one who suggested that kinky stuff," he reminded her, "but now that you have, I like the idea. I've definitely changed my mind about the zoo. I think we should just go back to bed. That'll be a *lot* more fun."

He could see she was fighting a smile. "And what if I don't *want* to go back to bed?"

He grinned. "How much do you want to bet I can change your mind in less than five minutes?"

She gave him a mock glare, then she grinned, too. "Never mind."

"Chicken," he said, poking her in the ribs.

In answer, she stuck out her tongue, then darted away when he tried to grab her. "Last one in the car is a monkey's uncle," she taunted, racing for the door.

Still laughing, Luke sprinted after her.

Clem was a good sport, he decided later. Although she'd professed not to be very excited by the idea of going to the zoo, she certainly acted as if she were having a wonderful time.

"What do you suppose those bears are thinking?" she mused as they leaned over an iron railing and watched two black bears sitting in a puddle of sun. She reached into her bag of popcorn and popped some into her mouth.

Luke grinned and put his arm around her shoulders. Her arms felt warm from the sun, and she smelled of fresh air and soap. "They're probably thinking how silly we look standing here staring at them."

She laughed, but a few minutes later her face fell into sober lines again. "It must be terrible to be penned up that way."

Luke shrugged. "They have a pretty good life."

"Well, *I'd* hate it," Clem said. "In fact, I can't imagine anything worse than not being free."

"These are animals, Clem, not human beings," he remarked reasonably, "and they are well taken care of. In fact, they receive better care here than they could ever achieve on their own."

Her gaze was speculative as she turned it his way. "Even so, don't you think freedom of choice is more important than being taken care of?"

"That depends."

"On what?"

"On whether the person . . . or animal . . . is capable of taking care of itself. You wouldn't expect a baby to assume control of its life, would you?"

"Well, no," she answered, "but these are adult animals. They take care of their babies the way they're supposed to until it's time to turn them loose, then they show them how to be independent. That's the natural order of things. For animals as well as humans."

"I agree that in an ideal world that's the way it would work, but this is reality, Clem."

"Well, what about humans? Surely you'll agree that freedom is the most basic and important element in a human life."

She was so passionate about the things she believed in. It was refreshing to find someone who cared so much, but in lots of ways he considered her to be naive in her idealism. He knew she would be furious if he were to tell her so, though, or to show her that her zeal amused him. She'd made it clear how she felt about people who didn't take her seriously.

"Well," he said slowly, "I agree that a free society—with freedom of speech, freedom of religion, all those freedoms in the Bill of Rights—*is* the most important and basic element in our lives. But that doesn't mean we can do whatever we want to do whenever we want to do it. After all, our society works only when people follow the rules, whether they are God's rules or man's rules...or our own personal moral code." He leaned against the fence separating them from the bears. "Sometimes that code can trap us just as effectively as these fences trap the animals."

Perhaps it was something in his voice. Perhaps it was something in his stance. Whatever it was, Clem's reporter instincts picked up on it because she immediately pounced. "Is that the way you feel? Trapped?"

Immediately he could have kicked himself for saying what he'd said. He certainly didn't want Clem feeling sorry for him.

He shrugged. "Sometimes." His gaze met hers. "Listen, forget it. I don't want to talk about this on such a nice day." He purposely lightened his voice. "Besides, I thought we weren't supposed to be serious."

"We're not supposed to get serious about each *other*. We can talk about serious subjects, though."

"Fine, but not now, okay?" He smiled. "Why don't we walk over to see the monkeys? They're always fun."

"No, Luke, come on," she insisted. "Finish what you were saying. Why do you feel trapped?"

"Clem . . ."

"I'm not budging from this spot until you tell me. Especially after seeing what a fantastic photographer you are. I want to know why you're not pursuing photography as a living."

He sighed. She wasn't going to give up until he gave her an answer. "Isn't it obvious? Every damned one of my brothers and now my sister look to me to keep the business running smoothly and making lots of money so that they can all live their lives without worry and do their own thing. So I can't leave."

"That's ridiculous. Of course you can."

"Clem, you don't understand."

"Look, Luke, it's been my experience that if someone really wants to do something, they'll find a way to do it. When they say they can't do something—for whatever reason—what it really means is they just don't want to badly enough to find a way."

Luke stiffened. "You don't know what you're talking about, Clem. You have no idea what the situation is."

"Sure I do. You felt as if you had to take your father's place when he died. And that was fine and admirable. After all, your brothers and sister were minors. But they're all grown-up now. Perfectly capable of taking care of themselves. And yet you continue to make things easy for them. Don't you know that unless you force them to stand on their own two feet, they never will?"

"That's easy for you to say. You're not the one who'll have to live with himself if the business fails."

"Don't you think you're being a little melodramatic about it? Surely the business won't collapse if you leave it to pursue your own interests."

"No one else understands or even has an interest in running the company."

Her expression was amused. "Well, no wonder. As long as Papa Luke, the martyr, continues to slave away—"

"A martyr! Is that what you think I am?"

"Can you think of a better description?"

Luke stared at her. It was one thing to be opinionated. It was quite another to be so smugly sure you were right about everything. And not only smug, but laughing at him! Finding the situation amusing! All his pleasure in the day, all his pleasure in her company, faded. Clenching his jaw, he said, "It must be wonderful to go through life knowing you have all the answers."

For just a second uncertainty clouded her eyes, then she gave a funny little offhand laugh. "Oh, come on, Luke. Lighten up. You're not *mad,* are you? Just because I pointed out the obvious?"

"No, I'm not mad," he lied. "But I am tired of this discussion. C'mon, let's go." He began to walk up the path.

She sprinted to catch up. "I think you are mad." When he didn't answer, she added defensively, "I only spoke the truth, Luke."

He stopped abruptly, rounding on her. "Well, I didn't ask for your opinion, did I? In fact, I didn't even want to talk about this. You're the one who forced the discussion." He looked at his watch. It was two o'clock. "Look, it's getting late. I need to get home. I have a lot of things to do, and I'm sure you do, too."

She stared at him.

He knew what she was thinking. They'd been supposed to have dinner together, and earlier he'd hoped she would want to spend the night again. But now everything had changed.

For a minute he thought she was going to say something else, but she didn't. A strained silence simmered between them as they walked to the car, and continued unrelieved during the twenty-minute drive to his house, where Clem had left her things. Cold anger and something else—something that throbbed deep inside—kept Luke's jaw taut and his eyes straight ahead. Once they reached the house they climbed out of the car separately and silently.

Several times while she was gathering her belongings and putting them into her suitcase, Luke thought she was going to apologize.

But she didn't.

And there was no way Luke was going to. No, she was the one who had caused this rift, and if it was going to be repaired, she should be the one to repair it.

Besides, she *owed* him an apology. She'd stuck her nose into a place it didn't belong, offered an opinion that was not only uneducated but totally unwanted, and in the process she'd let him know exactly what she thought of him.

Fine. If that was the way she felt, it was good he'd found out.

Still maintaining an icy silence, he drove her to her apartment. Once there, he pulled up in front of her building and parked at the curb. By the time he got out of the car and walked around to open the trunk and remove her suitcase, she had opened her own door and stood waiting on the sidewalk by the steps leading up to her floor.

She reached for the suitcase, and as he handed it to her, their gazes connected. She swallowed, the only outward indication that she was disturbed. "I—I had a great time," she finally said.

Luke nodded. *I had a great time, too, until you called me a martyr, among other things.* He could see that she wanted to make up, but he was still stung by her assessment of him.

"Do you want to go to Big Ed's tomorrow night?" she asked hopefully.

"Can't. I've got to work."

She nodded. "Well, maybe Tuesday night, then. I still—"

"I don't think so," he said, cutting her off. "I expect to be pretty busy from now on."

She stared at him, finally throwing up her hands and saying, "Oh, Luke, for heaven's sake! Quit acting like a big baby!"

Fury wiped out the regret he had begun to feel. Wiped out everything except a desire to hurt her the same way she'd hurt him. "Big baby, huh? Well, considering your low opinion of me, I'm sure you want nothing more to do with me, so let's call this goodbye, Miss Bennelli. It's been . . . illuminating."

He turned on his heel, stalked to his car and drove away without a backward glance.

Clem stared disbelievingly after his taillights. Her heart still hammered in shock at the stunning turn of events. Good grief! she thought. What is *wrong* with him? Couldn't the man take a little honest criticism?

What had he expected her to do? Lie? Yeah, right, she thought as she pounded angrily up the stairs and unlocked her apartment. That's exactly what he'd expected. Total agreement. Unconditional approval.

She walked inside and dropped her suitcase. Well, if that's what he wanted, maybe Clem was better off without him.

Let him sulk. Who cared? Who needed him? Clem certainly didn't.

For the next week Luke tried to put Clem out of his mind. He told himself he was better off without her. He told himself she was everything he'd first thought, and more.

Opinionated.

Noisy.

A smart ass.

And a royal pain in the butt.

And yet . . . unbidden, unwanted, images of her continued to intrude all week long. At the most inopportune times he would think of her the way she looked at the wedding. Laughing. Filled with joy and achingly lovely in her exuberance.

Or he'd see her in his bed. Rosy from their lovemaking. Warm and sweet and oh, so irresistible.

Each time he pushed the images away.

The last thing he needed or wanted in his life was someone so disruptive. Sure, they were great together in bed. Sure, she was lots of fun. Sure, they'd had some great times.

But he had no intention of ever calling her again. In fact, the only way he'd even talk to her again was if she called him.

For the next week Clem tried to put Luke out of her mind. It was hard, though. The oddest things reminded her of him. Green lights made her think of his eyes. The smell of coffee reminded her of the night they'd first made love. Church bells in the distance brought back reminders of the wedding and how Luke had looked standing at the front of St. Basil's.

And the ache in the vicinity of her heart was a constant reminder of the way he'd filled up the spaces in her life she hadn't even realized had been empty.

She missed him more than she'd ever imagined she would. She told herself he'd get over being mad. She told herself he hadn't meant it when he'd said goodbye. She told herself it was good he was gone, because his absence left her free to concentrate on work and the trial, which had begun in earnest.

All week the prosecution trotted out their witnesses and presented their case, and Clem made the most of unfolding events. She got lots of coverage at five, six and ten o'clock. She should have been deliriously happy, but she couldn't help remembering that it was Luke who had been responsible for her change in fortune.

And you repaid him by insulting him, a little voice inside her whispered.

Each night she hoped he would call, and each night her phone remained ominously silent.

By Thursday she was beginning to think maybe she owed Luke an apology. Maybe she really had been out of line, the way he'd seemed to think.

Maybe she should call him.

Friday morning Clem awakened with a stopped-up nose and scratchy throat. "Oh, great," she muttered, throwing off her covers. "Just what I need!"

By ten o'clock her head was pounding, and she knew she wasn't going to last the day. Thank God Judge Pollock must have felt the same way, because he banged his gavel down at noon and barked, "Court's recessed for the weekend. We'll resume at nine o'clock Monday morning."

By two, Clem's taping was squeaky-clean and ready to air, and she left a note for Raymond, who had already gone to lunch. It said, "I'm not feeling well. Going home to fight off this cold. Clem."

By 2:30 p.m. she was unlocking her apartment. She headed straight for the kitchen, where she found the aspirin. After downing two with a big glass of juice, she undressed—throwing her clothes anywhere they landed—pulled on an oversize T-shirt, closed the blinds and crawled into her still-unmade futon.

Within minutes she was asleep.

Clem knew she was dreaming. But the dream was so wonderful she didn't want to wake up.

In her dream she was lying with Luke in the middle of a sun-drenched meadow. They were snuggled close together, and every once in a while they'd kiss. The kisses sent little tingling sensations up and down her arms and legs and all over her body. He lazily caressed her, and the tingling sensations arrowed down to a common point.

She felt warm and happy and deliciously aroused.

She wanted to stay that way forever.

All Friday afternoon Luke thought about Clem. He wondered if maybe, just maybe, he had overreacted to what she had said.

After all, Clem always spoke her mind. And her opinions, even the ones he didn't agree with, usually amused him. Why hadn't he just laughed off her remarks? Maybe he *had* acted like a big baby, just as she'd accused....

When Clem woke up, about seven that evening, she suddenly knew exactly what she needed to do.

She washed her face and took a couple more aspirin, then filled up the coffeemaker and plugged it in.

Once the coffee was made and she'd taken several fortifying swallows, she picked up the phone and dialed Luke's home number.

She got his answering machine.

"Luke," she said, "I was wrong. I'm sorry, and I hope you'll give me the chance to apologize in person. When you get this message, I hope you'll call me." Then, taking a deep breath, she added, "I've missed you. A lot."

She hung up the phone slowly.

She'd done what she could.

The next move was up to him.

Chapter Eleven

Luke arrived home at ten—exhausted and wanting nothing more than to have a cold beer, then sink into the Jacuzzi and stay there for at least an hour.

Wearily he headed straight for the kitchen, where he removed a can of beer from the refrigerator. He popped the top, took a long, satisfying swallow, then headed for his answering machine.

The message light was blinking rapidly, indicating there were several calls.

The first two were from sales types, the third was from his mother. And then, startling him so that he nearly choked on his beer, Clem's voice saying, "Hi, Luke, sorry to miss you, but..."

He listened to her apology, feeling better by the minute, and when she got to the end and said she'd missed him—a lot—he slowly smiled, his exhaustion forgotten.

Two seconds later he was dialing her number.

"Clem?"

"Luke?" She sounded funny, not like herself at all.

"I just got your message." He sank onto the couch and propped his feet on the coffee table. "I was really glad to hear from you."

She sighed. "All this week I've been thinking about what happened between us, and I realized you were right. You didn't ask for my opinion, and I had no business inflicting it on you. I know how much I hate it when my family tries to tell me what to do, and here I was doing the same thing."

"Thanks," he said softly, "but I've been thinking, too, and I think you were right about the way I behaved. I *was* acting pretty juvenile."

"Well..."

"Well..."

They both laughed in embarrassment.

"I feel awkward," he said. "I don't know why."

"I know. Me, too," she admitted.

"Why do you sound so funny?"

"Funny? Oh, I've got a summer cold. God, I hate being sick!"

He laughed. "I'll bet you do." After a moment his voice sobered, and he said, "I missed you this week."

"Did you?" she asked softly.

He closed his eyes. "Yes."

"I'm glad."

"I wish you were here right now."

"No, you don't. You don't want to catch my cold."

"Maybe by tomorrow you'll be feeling better. But even if you aren't, I'll take my chances. How about it? You free tomorrow night?"

"Yes."

He smiled. "Good."

They made arrangements for him to pick her up about six the following evening, and then they hung up.

For the first time in a week Luke had no trouble sleeping.

On Monday, though, Luke had cause to remember his argument with Clem, because he could no longer postpone giving Rebecca an answer about whether or not he would buy out her share of the company.

"Well?" she asked eagerly, sitting down in front of his desk. "What's the verdict? Will you do it?"

The expression on her face told Luke she had no expectation of disappointment. He grimaced mentally. He had never let her down. "The only way I could buy you out would be to sell my house or cash in some of my investments," he said slowly.

She nodded. "Oh, I knew you couldn't just hand over the money this minute. I figured it would take time—"

"Rebecca."

She stopped. Frowned slightly.

"I'm not sure I want to do either of those things," he said firmly.

She bit her bottom lip. Storm clouds darkened her eyes. "Oh."

He sighed. "Look, I know you're disappointed. But give me some time to see what I can arrange, okay?

Maybe Doc or Alex would be interested in owning part of the company." Doc Owens and Alex Costas were ex-cops and old friends of his father. They'd been with the company since its inception. "And if they aren't, maybe the company could float you a loan."

The storm clouds disappeared and sunny skies reigned once more as her green eyes lit up happily. "Oh, that's great, Luke! I knew I could count on you." She grinned. "Let's start advertising for someone to fill my job right away, okay?"

After she left his office Luke thoughtfully rolled his pen between his fingers. Then he picked up his phone and dialed John's extension. Might as well talk about John's request, too, especially since the conversation with Rebecca had given him an idea.

Fifteen minutes later John breezed into his office. "What's up?" he said, sinking into the same chair Rebecca had vacated earlier.

"At the wedding you mentioned wanting to cut out fieldwork," Luke reminded him. "And I've been thinking that's not a bad idea."

"Great!"

"In fact, I'd like to do something different myself, so I thought I could start training you to take over—"

"Whoa! Wait a minute," John said, sitting up straight. "I don't want *your* job. God, that's all I'd need, all kinds of emergencies and having to stay late at night. No, I was thinking more in terms of taking over Rebecca's job when she leaves."

"But John, you're not a bookkeeper—"

"I wasn't a security expert, either, but I learned that job, and I'm sure as hell not a manager, and you seem to think I could learn how to do that,'' John noted reasonably.

Luke sighed. Of course, John was right. He could learn to do Rebecca's job, and with the responsibilities of his children, he was not a good candidate for taking over management of the company. Wryly, Luke thought that if he was going to stop being a martyr, he would have to look elsewhere for his replacement. "You're right...of course you are. How's this? As soon as I can get another agent hired to take your place, Rebecca can start training you."

John grinned. "Thanks, Luke. I knew you'd understand."

After John left Luke just sat there. *I knew you'd understand.* The words mocked him. Oh, sure, he understood, all right. He understood that with every passing day the hole he'd dug for himself was getting deeper and deeper.

The rest of May and the month of June flew by. Clem was satisfyingly busy at work covering the Spinosa trial, and she spent all of her free time with Luke.

She smiled every time she thought about him.

She loved being with him. He was a great companion and a terrific lover and he made no demands on her. What more could she ask for?

Of course, she wished he had more free time to spend with her, but when they *were* together, they did all kinds of fun things. They went to movies and out to dinner. They played dozens of games of pool and had a running bet going. Luke managed to get a weekend free the first week of June, and they drove to San Antonio and did the whole tourist thing. They even went to Astroworld one Saturday and rode every single roller coaster at least once and several of them two or three times. Clem laughed so hard she got the hiccups.

And Clem spent a lot of nights at Luke's house. She got so she just left a nightshirt, toothbrush, clean underwear and a change of clothing there all the time.

They talked a lot.

And they made love a lot.

Clem sighed with contentment just thinking about how good the lovemaking was. It was incredibly satisfying—the best sex she'd ever had—and the funny thing was, she wasn't tired of it.

She'd expected the first flush of desire to fade after a while, but instead of fading, it just seemed to grow stronger every day.

If anything, she wanted Luke more now than she had in the beginning.

Several times she'd thought what a shame it was she wasn't interested in any kind of permanent relationship, because if she had been, Luke would have been the perfect choice. He was as busy as she was, so he wasn't possessive about her time. He was intelligent, sexy, funny, and he had a strong sense of responsibility.

Too strong, actually, but after that disastrous day at the zoo she'd made herself a promise that she would not poke her nose into his family or business affairs again, and she hadn't, even though she was dying to know what he'd decided about Rebecca and the proposed buyout.

Still, no matter how perfect a candidate for a permanent relationship Luke was, she simply couldn't be interested. If she was tied to a serious relationship, how could she pick up and take off when her big break came?

And she was certain it *would* come. When a person wanted something as much as she wanted this, and when a person had worked as hard as she'd worked, her opportunity was bound to present itself. The only question was when.

Even so—as sure as she was that eventually she'd get a shot at something major like a network job, and as sure as she was that she would eventually be severing her relationship with Luke—she couldn't help but feel a strange kind of desolation every time she thought about going off and never seeing him again.

Each time this happened, she quickly shook off the alien emotion. She lectured herself.

Remember, Clem, what you and Luke agreed. You're just having fun together. You're each taking what you want now. That's it. No L words or M words or C words. Eventually, inevitably, you'll part. And when you do, it's going to be a clean break. No big emotional scene. And no regrets.

So life went on.

June ended, and with its passing, the Spinosa trial ground to a close with a conviction for Theresa Spinosa. Even the conviction carried controversy, because the sentence was death by injection, which many people objected to. Clem didn't allow her own beliefs to color her reporting, though, and her final report was picked up by the network feed and shown all over the country. Now would come the inevitable years-long round of appeals, but Clem's coverage of the trial was officially over.

July brought one-hundred-degree temperatures and hazy blue skies to Houston. People started making plans for the Fourth of July.

The Bennellis always had a big family get-together for the holiday. Clem debated skipping it this year but knew her family would be disappointed if she wasn't there. And she would be, too.

She actually enjoyed the blowout: all the kids running around wildly , the traditional foods like potato salad and baked beans and hot dogs and hamburgers cooked on the grill, the cold soft drinks and beer sitting in melting ice in the big cooler, the exuberant games of badminton and croquet in her parents' big, shady backyard, the homemade ice cream that her Aunt Florence always brought, and then—later—the whole gang trooping off to listen to music and watch the fireworks at Miller Outdoor Theater.

She hated to miss it, but Luke had mentioned doing something together, and if he was actually going to take the day off, she wanted to spend it with him. She wondered if she could risk inviting him to the family celebration, or would that cause too many comments?

Finally she decided she didn't care if an invitation to Luke *did* cause comments. Let her family talk all they wanted. Nothing would change. She and Luke would still know what their relationship was. All she really needed to do was warn Luke, and then the two of them could just take all comments in stride. In fact, they could laugh about them.

So she called Luke and invited him.

"Sounds like fun," he said. "I accept."

It *was* fun, in spite of the fact that in the first hour after their arrival her family ran pretty true to form. Her sisters kept sidling up to Clem and making sotto voce remarks like, "Boy, this looks like it's getting serious, Clem," and "You two sure are spending a lot of time together, aren't you?" and "Are we going to be hearing an announcement soon?"

"It's not serious at all," Clem said to Miranda, ignoring Miranda's amused expression. "Go back to playing kissy-face with your husband and quit worrying about me."

"Yes, we're having a great time," Clem answered Vanessa, acting as if she didn't see Vanessa's sly smile.

"I have no idea what you're talking about," Clem told Valerie, staring her straight in the eye even though Valerie continued to smile knowingly.

None of the remarks was made in Luke's hearing, of course, but Clem was sure he felt the vibes emanating from her eager-to-see-Clem-married sisters.

As Clem's father and brother Frank were taking the hot dogs and hamburgers off the grill, Clem found herself alone with her mother in the kitchen. Her mother said, "I'm glad you brought Luke today."

Clem nodded noncommittally.

"He's a fine man," her mother continued, eyeing Clem over the salad bowl she'd just removed from the refrigerator. When Clem didn't answer, she added, "You could do a lot worse."

Clem sighed noisily. "Yes, mother, I know, but I'm not serious about him."

For a few seconds her mother didn't say anything, just studied Clem's face. Then her mother sighed, too. "If you're not serious about him, why are you spending so much time with him?"

Clem considered saying, *Because the sex is fantastic,* but she knew she never would. Not only because she respected and loved her mother but because Clem knew, deep down, that an answer like that would not be the whole truth. In fact, it wouldn't even come close to being the truth.

Clem wasn't sure she knew what the truth was. She'd thought she knew, but sometimes lately she'd been having doubts. Fears, actually. Fears that maybe, just maybe, Luke was becoming too important to her.

So her answer to her mother was quiet and as honest as she could make it. "I like Luke a lot, that's why."

Her mother smiled. "That's a good beginning."

For the rest of the day Clem thought about her mother's words as she watched Luke with her family. He fit in as if he belonged there. He made easy conversation with her father and brothers as well as her mother and sisters. Everyone seemed to like him. Of course, since Mark was already a part of their family, they were predisposed to like him, but still . . .

Suddenly Clem realized just how much she would miss Luke when he was gone from her life.

Suddenly she began to think that maybe she didn't really want him gone from her life.

The thought frightened her, and she tried to shove it away. It refused to go.

Wasn't it ironic? she thought. Just as she'd found the kind of man and the kind of relationship she so loudly proclaimed she wanted, she wasn't sure it was what she wanted at all.

That night, lying in Luke's arms in his big bed, the thought that maybe she'd been wrong all these years, that maybe her sisters and her mother had been right—that all it would take to change Clem's mind about marriage and commitment was the right man—continued to haunt her.

And frighten her.

She closed her eyes, willing herself to go to sleep. She didn't want to think about this complication. She didn't want to think about anything.

And then, just as she had managed to clear her mind, just as she was drifting toward sleep, Luke said, "I had a great time today. You've got a nice family."

Clem sighed deeply. "Um, thanks."

He chuckled. "They sure do want to see you get married, don't they?"

Clem's heart skittered, and she opened her eyes. "Did they say something to you?"

"No, no," he protested. "It's just that the women kept watching me, and then they'd look at you. Anyway, it wasn't hard to figure out how their minds were working."

"It's never hard to figure out how their minds work," Clem said, giving her standard, slightly sarcastic answer, even though her heart wasn't in it. "That's because their minds are one-track."

He laughed again. "Don't be so hard on them, Clem. They're just normal women. *You're* the one who's different."

She stiffened, oddly hurt, even though for years she'd taken pride in the fact of her difference.

He nuzzled his mouth against the lobe of her ear. "Hey, don't get mad. I wasn't criticizing you. I was just stating a fact, that's all. Your family doesn't understand you." He took the lobe into his mouth and bit it gently. "I do."

I'm glad you do. You're about the only one around here who does.

Long after Luke had fallen asleep, Clem lay awake thinking. She had never expected her emotions to become engaged when she'd started seeing Luke. But they had. She wasn't sure exactly what she was feeling for him, but whatever it was, it was scary.

What should she do? Break off with him now, before she got in any deeper? Before she got so attached to him she'd end with a broken heart?

Cut her losses, so to speak.

Or should she stay the course? See this situation through to the end and take her lumps, whatever they were?

Unfortunately, no amount of thinking brought her any closer to an answer.

On Tuesday the station was all abuzz with the news that Houston had been chosen to be the site of a huge oil summit later that month. World leaders from all the industrialized nations as well as all the oil-producing nations would be attending, as would scores of reporters and journalists from all over the world. This summit was one of the most important events to happen in Houston in many years.

The minute Clem heard about it, she marched into Raymond's office.

He looked up from his work. As he did, his glasses slid farther down his nose.

"Raymond," she said without preamble, "I want to cover the summit."

He sighed and leaned back in his chair, in the process pushing his glasses up where they belonged. "Now wait a minute. Just because you did a good job with the Spinosa trial doesn't mean—"

"Good? I did a *great* job with the Spinosa trial," Clem interjected. "And you know it!" She gave him one of her meant-to-be-intimidating glares, which rarely worked with him, but she had to try.

Raymond stared at her, then slowly smiled.

Clem nearly fell over. Raymond *never* smiled.

"Okay, you did a great job," he conceded.

Holy cow. Maybe hell froze over, and I don't know it.

"But that doesn't mean you're going to get every plum assignment around here," he continued. Despite his answer, his voice was mild and the smile still hovered around his mouth.

"I don't see why not," Clem retorted, stunned but encouraged by his completely unexpected change of attitude. "I'm the best reporter you've got, and it's time you admitted it."

"The best, huh?"

"Yes." Really encouraged now, she perched on the end of his desk. "Come on, Raymond. I want this," she wheedled.

"Charles wants it, too. He was in here earlier, and I told him I hadn't decided who would get the assignment."

"I'll do a better job than Charles."

Raymond continued to eye her over the top of his glasses as he rolled a pencil between his fingers. The clock on the wall ticked away the seconds.

Clem held her breath.

Finally he said, "Okay, Bennelli, it's yours. But don't blow it!"

"That's terrific," Luke said that evening as they sat over the remains of their enchilada dinner. "I would guess this will be an even better opportunity than the Spinosa trial."

"Oh, boy, is it ever! And you could've knocked me over with a feather when Raymond was so agreeable. I'm still stunned." She grinned happily as she lifted her glass of iced tea and drained it.

"I don't see why. You did a great job on the trial, and he's finally realized how valuable you are." Luke was ashamed of himself, because his reaction to her announcement had produced mixed emotions. He was genuinely happy for her, but a little voice inside had reminded him that this assignment would bring her closer to the fulfillment of her goals and would therefore hasten the day she would leave Houston.

Leave him.

The knowledge sank into his gut like a brick. His emotions churned but he kept a pleased expression on his face. It wouldn't do to have her guess what he was thinking.

He didn't understand himself. Why was the idea of her leaving causing him such turmoil? Hadn't he always known she would leave? Hadn't they agreed, months ago, that this relationship of theirs was only temporary? That they were just having a good time together?

No L words. No M words. No C words.

Wasn't this no-promises, no-commitments relationship exactly what he had wanted?

Yes to all of the above.

So why, if that was true, was he troubled by the thought of losing her?

Because she's begun to mean more to you than you ever expected, stupid.

"C'mon," Clem said, obviously unaware of his turbulent thoughts. "I challenge you to a couple of games of pool at Big Ed's. I feel like celebrating."

"I can think of better things to do to celebrate than playing pool," Luke responded automatically, but his mind was still churning.

"We'll do those things later," Clem promised, smiling.

Luke swallowed. When she smiled at him like that, it did something to the vicinity around his heart. Made him feel something he had never expected to feel.

Wasn't it ironic, he thought later, after they'd played a couple of games of pool and come back to his home and his bed and made urgent, passionate love to one another, that now that he'd found exactly the type of woman and the type of relationship he'd always believed he wanted, he was no longer sure he did?

The next morning, as they both prepared for their respective work days, Clem said, "You know, from now until the summit is over, I'm not going to be able to spend much time with you. Probably only weekends."

Luke, who had just finished shaving and was getting ready to take his shower, replied, "Don't worry about it. I've been taking too much time off lately, anyway."

Later, after Clem had gone and Luke was on his way to his office, he thought about how hard he'd tried to change his life in the past month, and yet nothing had significantly changed.

None of his brothers was interested in learning his job. In fact, lately Matthew had been making noises about getting out of the business altogether.

At least the situation with Rebecca and John had worked out satisfactorily. Alex Costas had eagerly bought out Rebecca's share, and John had proven to be a quick study as far as Rebecca's job went. Luke had also been successful in replacing John in the field.

But none of these satisfying results would help Luke achieve his own goals. Unfortunately, he was no closer to being able to leave the business himself than he had been before. And at the rate he was going, he might never be.

For the next week Luke worked long hours and managed to clear out some things that had been hanging over his head for months. And then, eight days after Clem had told him about landing the summit assignment, he received a call from a former client who asked him if his firm could provide some additional security for Tomas Chimensky, who would attend the summit as a representative of one of the Balkan countries. Luke's former client said there had been a threat to Chimensky's life, and his supporters felt additional security was warranted.

Luke gladly accepted. This was one of the most interesting jobs to come his way in a long time. Besides, being there would give him an opportunity not only to watch Clem work but to keep an eye on her.

Luke hadn't told Clem, but it worried him a little that she was going to be participating in the summit. A meeting such as this one would attract all kinds of radicals and fringe groups, and who knew what kind of danger she would be in? He decided he would personally handle the security for Tomas Chimensky.

During the two weeks after receiving the summit assignment, Clem managed to push her unsettling thoughts and unanswered questions regarding Luke from her mind. At least most of the time. The reason she was mostly successful at doing so was the monumental amount of research necessary if she was going to cover the summit successfully and intelligently.

Clem never did anything halfway, and the summit was the most important story she had been assigned so far. This was her big opportunity. She intended to do a spectacular job. A memorable job. The kind of job that would bring her to the attention of the bigwigs at network headquarters.

She threw herself into her preparation, even as she handled routine daily assignments. A lot of her work had to be done on her own time, which left even fewer hours to be with Luke.

But that was okay. In fact, considering how she'd been feeling lately, maybe maintaining some distance from him was the best thing for her.

But no matter how hard Clem worked in preparation for the summit, she couldn't completely banish her problem regarding Luke from her mind.

Finally, in desperation, she called Annie. "I don't suppose you could come into town and meet me for lunch tomorrow?" she asked.

"I'd love to," Annie said.

They made arrangements to meet at their favorite restaurant from college days—a small neighborhood soup-and-sandwich place near Rice University—where they knew they'd have privacy and be allowed to sit as long as they liked without feeling as if they had to leave.

Annie was prompt, as usual. And, also as usual, she looked smashing in a turquoise sundress and matching sandals. Clem looked down at her own hastily donned outfit of khaki walking shorts and plain white blouse and mentally grimaced. She should take more care with her clothes.

The friends hugged, then slid into their booth. After placing identical orders of baked potato soup and half a club sandwich, Annie said, "Okay, spill it."

Clem smiled. "You know me pretty well, don't you?"

"I certainly know you well enough to know you wouldn't call and ask me to meet you for lunch unless you had something on your mind you wanted to talk about." Annie waited a moment, then added, "Is it Luke?"

Clem sighed, then nodded. "I don't know what to do about him."

"Why don't you tell me what the problem is, and maybe I can help?" Annie suggested gently, her eyes warm and sympathetic and filled with reminders of their long friendship.

Clem fiddled with her paper napkin, finally raising her eyes to meet Annie's gaze. "I think I'm in love with him." Saying the words out loud caused Clem's heart to beat faster.

Annie smiled. "I could've told you that weeks ago."

"How could you know it weeks ago when I only discovered it recently myself?"

Annie shrugged. "I know you, that's all. I could see what was happening even if you couldn't."

Clem nodded glumly.

"I don't understand what the problem is," Annie continued. "Luke is obviously crazy about you, too, so why the long face?"

"First of all, I'm not as sure as you are that Luke is 'crazy about me,' as you put it. Secondly, I don't need this kind of thing in my life."

Annie chuckled. "Good grief, Clem, you act like being in love is comparable to having the chicken pox, or something."

"It's worse. At least with the chicken pox you're back to normal in a few weeks."

Annie shook her head. "You're impossible. Most women would kill to be involved with a man like Luke, and you're moaning about it. Tell me why being in love with him is such a bad thing.''

''Because...'' Clem took another deep breath. ''Because the relationship can't go anywhere.''

''Why not?''

Just then their waitress came with their bowls of soup, and Clem waited until she'd gone before answering Annie. ''Because I'm outta here when my break comes. You know that, Annie. Shoot, I've been working toward a network slot or something like that for years now. I'm sure not going to let a man stand in the way of my future.''

''Oh? Does that mean you intend to walk off and leave Luke? Despite being in love with him?''

Clem frowned. ''I don't know. I'm not sure I can.''

Annie smiled. ''Well, good. That's a start, anyway. Seems to me the next step is to talk to Luke about the way you feel. The two of you can work something out.''

''I can't talk to Luke.''

Annie, who had been about to take a spoonful of soup, put her spoon back in the bowl. ''For heaven's sake, Clem, why on earth not?''

''Because we have a deal.''

''A deal? What kind of a deal?''

So Clem told Annie all about her understanding with Luke, finishing by saying, ''He was very clear about it. We even shook hands on the whole thing. There were to be no words like *love, marriage* or *commitment.* Period.''

''Well, you changed your mind,'' Annie noted, ''so maybe he's changed his, too.''

"I don't think so. He's had plenty of opportunity to say so, and he hasn't."

"Maybe he feels the same hesitance you do."

"For the sake of argument, let's say he *had* changed his mind. How would that solve anything? We'd still have the dilemma of me leaving here eventually."

Annie nodded and resumed eating her soup. "I don't know what the answer is, Clem. All I'm saying is, it's stupid not to talk about it."

Now it was Clem's turn to nod. She took spoonful of her soup, too. A few seconds later she met Annie's gaze. "I'm afraid to bring the subject up." Once the words were spoken, Clem realized how true they were.

"Oh, Clem," Annie said softly. "Why?"

Clem swallowed. "What if he says he thinks it'll be best to call it quits right now?"

"I don't think that's going to happen."

"But what if it *does?*" Clem said. "What if it does? After all, no matter what you think Luke's feelings are, there are no guarantees."

"No, there aren't," Annie agreed. "But I've never known you to avoid something because it might turn out unpleasantly. The Clem I know faces every challenge with her head held high."

Clem stared at her friend for a long moment. Then she smiled. "Damn you, Annie."

Annie smiled back. "You're welcome."

Chapter Twelve

Clem gave a lot of thought to Annie's advice, but she decided that, as sensible as it was, she simply wasn't ready for a showdown with Luke. Because no matter what Annie thought about him and his feelings toward Clem, Clem wasn't so confident.

As she'd told Annie, Luke had had ample opportunity to declare a change of heart, and he hadn't. If Clem pressured him, he might get nervous and decide it was time to call it quits. And right now, with all the stress of preparing for the summit, Clem didn't think she could handle the additional emotional upheaval of a break with Luke.

So she decided she would wait to confront him until after the summit was over. Once her decision was made, she felt better, and she threw herself back into her preparations for the summit with renewed energy.

Dignitaries from participating countries started arriving in Houston a few days before the summit was slated to begin, and as each one appeared Clem and her crew were there. She managed to snag interviews with several of the top representatives, and on the eve of the summit one of her interviews was shown on the network's evening news, right after the national anchor's coverage was aired. Clem was thrilled, and she could hardly sleep that night.

The day of the opening session dawned hazy and humid, with the weathermen predicting that the mercury would top 105 degrees. Clem was awake by five, showered and dressed by six and at the station by six-thirty.

Although for the past forty-eight hours she'd been working around the clock, snatching a few hours' sleep here and there, and should have been exhausted, she didn't feel tired this morning. In fact, she felt invigorated.

Even her ongoing dilemma over Luke, which had caused her so much turmoil in recent weeks, had been relegated to the back of her mind.

Maybe that was the solution, she thought wryly. Work, work and more work. When she was this busy, she had very little time to worry about anything.

As she prepared for the day, she decided she would focus her efforts on getting some kind of interview with Tomas Chimensky. Of all the participants, he was the most controversial right now, and therefore the most interesting and newsworthy.

At eight o'clock she and her crew, including Jason Ruggerio, whom she was beginning to think of as her personal cameraman, had joined the other media just outside the doors of Hammon Hall on the grounds of Rice University, Clem's alma mater, the site of the summit.

Clem waited impatiently for the first arrivals. The welcome speech, which would be given by the senior senator from Texas, was scheduled for nine o'clock. Most of the spectators holding coveted attendance tickets were already there and waiting. Clem figured the main participants wouldn't begin to arrive until just before the start of the session.

As the minutes ticked closer to eight-thirty, the crowd of sightseers grew steadily. It amazed Clem to see so many children, many of whom carried balloons, flags and signs welcoming various representatives.

In addition to the sightseers and general wellwishers, there were also groups of demonstrators protesting everything from pollution of the environment to violation of human rights by participating countries. Clem considered abandoning her position to interview some of the protestors, but decided they could wait. She didn't want to take a chance on missing Chimensky, and the protestors would be there all day long, she was sure.

The first of the limousines pulled up to the curb a little after eight-thirty. For the next fifteen minutes Clem tried to get as many of the dignitaries on camera as she could manage. She grew adept at thrusting her microphone near their faces and firing off rapid questions. She'd learned a long time ago that the first couple of reporters who managed to do so were the most likely to get answers. After that, the people who were their objectives would start waving the reporters away.

So far, so good, she thought. She'd managed to beat out several of the other reporters and get responses from five or six of the more important dignitaries.

Around eight forty-five there was a lull for a few minutes. Clem used the break to survey the crowd. She grinned as she spotted Luke, who stood near the street. As always, her first sight of him after not seeing him for a while produced a flutter of butterflies in her stomach and a lilt to her heart.

He looked ten times better than most of the men around him, she thought. Today he was dressed in a dark gray suit, white shirt and dark striped tie. He had told her that on a job like this one, conservative business clothing helped him blend into the crowd. As she watched, his gaze roamed the crowd. He moved slowly toward the outside gates, and Clem knew Tomas Chimensky would arrive soon.

Motioning to Jason to follow her, Clem edged her way closer to Luke. He spotted her coming and frowned. Clem knew he probably wanted her to stay away because of the threat to Chimensky's life, but if something *did* happen here—which Clem seriously doubted—she sure as heck didn't intend to miss out on it, so she ignored his dark look and continued moving closer.

A large gray limousine pulled up to the curb, and Luke's attention turned to the new arrival. Clem pushed out toward the sidewalk, saying, "C'mon, Jason." This had to be Chimensky and his party, and she was determined to get him on camera.

A man emerged from the passenger side of the front of the limousine. His eyes scanned the crowd. When he saw Luke, he nodded, and Luke moved forward.

Amazing, Clem thought, noticing how the crowd parted for Luke, as if it sensed that he was somebody to reckon with. She inched closer until she was satisfied with her position. Chimensky would have to pass right by her as he entered the gates.

The man who had gotten out of the limousine first opened the back door. Several men Clem didn't recognize climbed out. She glanced at Jason, who was slightly behind her to her right. He was already filming.

Finally, Tomas Chimensky's distinctive head of thick gray curls and matching gray beard emerged from the limousine.

An excited murmur rippled through the onlookers. Clem, pulse quickening in excitement, was ready.

Chimensky, surrounded by his entourage of whom Luke was one, stepped onto the sidewalk and began walking up the path toward the gates leading to the building that was his destination.

As he drew abreast of her, she thrust her microphone toward him, saying, "Mr. Chimensky, Mr. Chimensky, do you hold out any hope that your relationship with Boris Katanya will improve as a result of the summit?" And then, just as he opened his mouth to answer, a loud popping noise erupted.

Two things happened almost simultaneously.

Chimensky was pushed down by his bodyguards.

And Luke tackled Clem.

Clem was so shocked she couldn't even yell. She landed facedown on the concrete, skinning her knees and the palms of her hands and losing her microphone in the process.

Bedlam exploded on all sides.

Shouts. Screams. People pushing.

Luke's weight pressed down on her.

Clem flailed at him uselessly. "Let me up!" she shouted.

"It was just a balloon popping," someone yelled close by. Others picked up the cry.

By the time Luke removed his body from hers and helped her to a standing position, the excited babble of the crowd had begun to die down.

Clem was furious. Her carefully chosen navy linen dress was soiled, her stockings had holes at both knees, her palms were stinging, she'd lost her microphone and, along with it, all chance of any kind of interview with Chimensky, who had already been whisked inside the building.

She wanted to kill Luke. Why had he knocked her down like that? She rounded on him, yelling, "Have you lost your mind? Look what you did to me! What did you think you were doing?"

His face was set in grim lines, his eyes unapologetic as they met hers. "I was trying to protect you. What did you *think* I was doing?"

"Protect me! From what?" Her voice trembled with rage and humiliation. Everyone was looking at them, and she could see some of the other reporters snickering behind their hands.

"From what I thought was a gunshot," he said through clenched teeth. Tight-lipped, he grabbed her upper arm and yanked her after him until they'd reached the perimeter of the crowd and had some measure of privacy. They stood only inches apart as they faced off. He was still gripping her arms. "Don't you realize what could have happened?" he growled. "I thought you were in danger. I was trying to keep you from being killed."

"And I was trying to do my job!" she shouted, not in any mood to be placated.

His hands tightened. For a moment she was afraid he was going to shake her. Then his grip and his expression softened. "Clem, I know you're angry and I even understand why, but you've got to understand something, too. I could no more have stopped myself from trying to protect you than I could stop breathing."

Clem nearly stopped breathing herself at the look in his eyes.

"I'm crazy about you, you idiot, and I was never so scared in my life in those seconds when I thought I might lose you," he said in a low, urgent voice.

Suddenly all Clem's anger evaporated. She stared at Luke, the realization of what he had just said drumming through her.

He'd said he was crazy about her! She didn't know whether to laugh or cry. She trembled, and whether it was a delayed reaction to the events of the past few minutes or to his unexpected declaration, she would never know.

"I—I don't know what to s-say," she finally stammered.

"Don't say anything right now. You've got to get back to work, and so do I. We'll talk later, okay?"

"Okay."

He gave her a quick hug. "Come to the house tonight when you're finished."

"Yes."

And then he was striding off, and Clem, senses still reeling, went to find her crew and repair the damage to her person.

For the rest of the day Luke had recurring flashes of fear each time he thought about what could have happened to Clem. In that instant when he'd thought her life was in danger, he'd realized that she meant more to him than anyone else in the world. He'd forgotten why he was there. He'd forgotten about Chimensky. He'd forgotten everything except Clem and protecting her.

Thank God nothing had happened.

Thank God she was all right.

But once his fear wore off and he began to think about the morning's events, he was filled with a new kind of trepidation. How would Clem react to his revelation that he loved her? Would she get scared and bolt?

The thought filled him with a new kind of fear.

He guessed he would find out tonight.

Clem didn't arrive at Luke's house until after midnight. She was exhausted yet exhilarated. After the fiasco where she'd tried to interview Chimensky and had gotten flattened by Luke instead, she'd cleaned herself up—sending Jason off to buy her some new panty hose—and waited for the noon break.

She was determined to get her interview.

She did.

Chimensky was one of the first group of attendees to exit the building on his way to the official luncheon. When Clem poked her microphone in his face, asking the same question she'd asked him that morning, he stopped and actually looked at her.

Then he smiled and courteously answered. He stood there for at least two minutes, answering several subsequent questions, as well.

Clem was elated.

After that she interviewed some of the marchers and protestors, then hurried back to the station to edit her film and get it ready for the five-o'clock news. Afterward, it was back to the university and the close of the day's session. Then more interviews, then back to the station again to prepare additional footage for the ten-o'clock news.

Finally, at close to midnight, she called it a day.

And now here she was, finally free to go to Luke's. As she got closer to his house, some of her elation over the day's successes receded, to be replaced with an unsettling flutter of nerves and trepidation.

What would happen tonight? That tonight was going to be pivotal to her relationship with Luke she had no doubt.

When she pulled in to his driveway he walked out to meet her, and her heartbeat accelerated. Before she had time to say more than "hi," he gathered her into his arms and kissed her hungrily.

By the time he let her up for air, her pulse was racing.

"I know we said no L words." His voice was rough with emotion. "But I don't care. I love you, Clem. I nearly lost it today when I thought you were in danger."

Her heart soared. "Oh, Luke. I—I love you, too."

He kissed her again, with a sweetness that touched Clem deeply. She clung to him, pouring her heart and soul into her response. She could feel his heart beating against hers, and she wished they could stay this way forever. She wished they never had to talk, never had to face the problems ahead of them.

Finally, though, they broke apart, and he said, "Let's go inside."

She nodded.

Holding hands, they walked into the house. In silent agreement they headed for the bedroom. Once there, he gently turned her to face him and kissed her again—a long, deep, hungry kiss that said all the things that hadn't yet been said aloud.

Clem gave herself up to the emotions pummeling her. She loved this man. She loved him with an intensity of which she'd never believed herself capable.

They kissed for a long time, and then, still without words, they undressed and climbed into Luke's big bed where they made slow, sweet, infinitely satisfying love to each other. Clem hadn't thought their lovemaking could get any better, but this time, this night, was an experience she couldn't have described with words.

It wasn't that Luke was any more skillful or that her responses were any more powerful—at least not in the physical sense. What was happening tonight was a sharing of each other that went beyond the physical. It touched her heart. And it touched her soul.

Instead of simply making love, they loved each other.

Afterward, they lay entwined, and Clem could hear and feel Luke's heart beating under her palm.

He kissed her forehead. "I love you, Clem."

Her arms tightened around him. "I love you, too."

"Do you want to talk about it now or wait until morning?"

She sighed. She felt so good. She didn't want the good feeling to go away. "Wait until morning," she said sleepily.

She felt his smile against her forehead. "Okay."

They kissed again, and then Clem snuggled against him and within moments was asleep.

The next morning Luke waited until they'd showered and dressed before suggesting that they have their coffee in the living room. Once they were seated next to each other on the couch, he said, "Okay, Clem. Time to talk, don't you think?"

She sighed. She couldn't postpone this indefinitely. "Yes, I guess so."

"What are we going to do about us?"

"I don't know."

He smiled crookedly. "Falling in love wasn't part of the deal, was it?"

She met his gaze. "No... no, it wasn't."

"So back to my question. What are we going to do about it now that we have?"

Something about his tone stiffened her spine, causing her hackles to rise a bit. "Why are you asking me? Isn't this a mutual problem?"

He shrugged, then took a swallow of his coffee. "You're the one who wants to be a world news correspondent, not me. You've made it clear that you plan to leave Houston the first chance you get. Well, like it or not, I'm stuck here. So where does that leave us?"

Clem hesitated. She'd told herself she would stay away from the subject of his relationship with his family. Still, all the rules had changed now, hadn't they? And he'd asked her. "Why are you stuck here?"

"Let's not play games, Clem. You know why. We've talked about this before, remember? The business is here. The business that supports my family."

"It would still support your family if someone else was running it."

"It's not that simple."

"It seems pretty simple to me."

"That's because you're not involved. There *is* no one else to run the business. Believe me, I've tried, but none of my brothers are interested."

"How have you tried?"

"I've talked to each of them individually. They've made it very clear how they feel. They all say basically the same thing. They have no interest in management and no desire to spend the kind of time and effort it requires to run the company."

"And you accepted that."

His jaw hardened. "What else could I do? I can't *force* them to do something they don't want to do."

"Oh? Looks to me as if they're forcing *you* to do something you say you don't want to do."

For a long moment it was very quiet in the room.

"You don't understand," he finally said.

"Oh, I think I do. Your family has been taking advantage of your skewed sense of duty for so long, they think this is the way things are supposed to be." She refrained from using the word *martyr,* knowing it would only inflame him. And she didn't want to make him angry. She just wanted him to open his eyes and *see.* "Luke, they can't take advantage of you if you don't let them. I think if you really want to leave, all you have to do is pack your bags and go."

"And what if the business collapses?"

"Oh, come on. Do you really think that'll happen?"

"It could."

"Well, if it does, that's their problem, not yours."

He stared at her. "You know, Clem, I don't think I ever realized just how selfish and self-centered you are until today."

Clem stared at him for a long moment. "I might be self-centered, Luke, but at least I'm not afraid to go after what I want. And you know what? I think you are. I think, no matter what you say about duty and responsibility, the plain truth is you're scared to pursue your dream, because maybe, just maybe, you won't be good enough."

* * *

"Oh, Clem! How could you say that?" Annie demanded.

"I don't know," Clem replied morosely. It was midafternoon, and Clem hadn't been able to think of anything but the horrible scene with Luke that morning and the way it had ended, with both of them stiff and hurt and angry. "It made me mad when he called me selfish."

"I'm sure it did," Annie said. "But what you said back to him was much, much worse."

Clem sighed heavily. "I know."

"You as much as called him a coward! Honestly, Clem, you're impossible."

"I know," Clem said again.

"Well, what're you going to do now? Apologize?"

"Oh, Annie, what's the use?"

"The use!" Annie exclaimed. "You love him! He loves you! You can't just toss that away. So you said some hurtful things to each other. So what? It probably won't be the last time."

Clem sighed again and doodled on her scratch pad. "But it's so hopeless. Because he was right. I *am* leaving here if I get the opportunity, and where does that leave us? He's obviously not going to even consider changing his life. He said it himself. He's stuck here in Houston."

"But, Clem—"

"Oh, God, Annie, no wonder I never wanted to fall in love! Love just makes you miserable!"

At four o'clock Clem's phone rang.

She lifted the receiver. "Clem Bennelli."

"Miss Bennelli, this is Jake Webster with WNN in Chicago."

Clem's heart jumped. "Uh, yes, hello, Mr. Webster," she managed to say without sounding too goofy, although excitement caused her hand to tremble as she automatically picked up a pencil to make notes.

"I saw some of your coverage of the Theresa Spinosa trial. You did a great job."

Clem swallowed. "Thank you." Jake Webster of Worldwide News Network! She could hardly believe it.

"And congratulations. You certainly scooped our man in Houston with your interview of Tomas Chimensky."

"Thanks," Clem said again. Then, recovering some of her poise, she added, "I was pretty proud of that interview." What did Webster want with her? Could he possibly...? The thought trailed off, too exciting to even put into words.

"Are you interested in a job with more scope and opportunity than the one you've got at KTEX?" he asked bluntly.

Clem stopped breathing.

"Because we've got an opening here at WNN, and I think you're the person to fill it."

Oh, my god. Her heart was pounding. "I'm *very* interested," she replied, hoping she sounded cool, hoping Jake Webster couldn't tell that she was so excited she was about to faint.

"Good," he said. "Can you come to Chicago on Thursday so we can talk about it?"

"You name the time. I'll be there," Clem promised.

When she eventually hung up the phone, she just sat there, stunned.

This was it.

The break she'd been waiting for.

And then, in a rush, memories of last night clouded her excitement. She closed her eyes. Oh, God. Luke.

What would happen to her and Luke now?

Luke snapped at everyone all day long. He couldn't get Clem's taunts out of his mind. *Maybe you're afraid. Maybe you think you won't be good enough.* She'd made him furious when she'd said those things. And she was wrong! She was dead wrong! If one of his brothers were to walk in here now and say he'd changed his mind, he wanted Luke's job, Luke would be out of here so fast it would make Clem's head spin!

By the middle of the afternoon most of his employees were giving him a wide berth. About four-thirty Rebecca poked her head around the corner of his office doorway. "Hey, Luke, busy?"

He looked up. "Sort of." He hoped she'd take the hint. He wasn't in the mood to talk to anyone, not even Rebecca.

But she didn't. She walked in, shut the door behind her and perched on the edge of his desk. "What's wrong?" she asked, her green eyes soft and concerned.

"Nothing." He avoided her eyes.

"Oh, come on, Luke, I know you better than that. Something's bothering you. If you'd tell me what it is, maybe I could help."

He looked down at the report on his desk. "No one can help."

"Luke..."

He sighed, raising his eyes to meet her gaze. "Look, Rebecca, I know you mean well, but I don't want to talk about this, okay?"

After a few moments she nodded. "Okay." She stood. "But if you do, my door is always open." Then she smiled. "Well, it'll only be open another week, because John is pretty much ready to take over my job completely."

He forced a smile. "Thanks. I appreciate your concern."

She hesitated, then walked around the desk and leaned down to hug him. "Don't mention it."

After she left, Luke got up and shut his office door. Then he walked to the window and looked out. His office building was located on the Katy Freeway near Antoine, only a ten-minute drive from his house. He stared at the bumper-to-bumper westbound traffic as it snaked along.

What was he going to do?

You know what you should do. You should call Clem and apologize. This time what happened was your fault. If you hadn't called her selfish, she never would have suggested you were a coward.

His accusation was wrong. Clem wasn't selfish. Just because she was single-minded about achieving her goals didn't mean she didn't care about others.

He had always known where she stood. She'd made her position perfectly clear. It wasn't fair of him to get so angry with her because she was acting the way she'd always acted.

She hadn't changed.

He had.

The question was, was her assessment of him right? Although he'd been stomping around all day telling himself she was wrong about him, was she?

Was there truth in what she'd said? *Was* he afraid to go for the gold?

Were all his reasons about why he couldn't leave the company to give his photography a shot simply excuses?

Right now he didn't know.

But he guessed that if he and Clem were to have any kind of chance together he'd better find out.

Clem's phone rang just as she was getting ready to leave for the day.

Mind still churning over the unexpected call from Jake Webster, she distractedly answered, "Clem Bennelli."

"Calling me a coward was a low blow."

Her heart skipped. It was Luke! "I didn't call you a coward."

"Sure you did."

"Oh, Luke, I'm sorry. You know me. I've got such a big mouth. I'm always popping off without thinking."

"It's not your fault. I asked for it. I should never have called you selfish."

She smiled. "Maybe you were right."

He was silent for so long she thought maybe he'd hung up. Then he said, "I love you, Clem."

Sudden tears stung her eyes. "I love you, too," she whispered. *Oh, Luke, Luke, what are we going to do?*

"I'm sorry about this morning."

"I am, too." What would he say when he found out about Jake Webster's call?

"Do you think we can talk about this without losing our tempers again?"

She forced a chuckle, blinking away the tears. "It'll be a challenge."

His answering chuckle gave her a bittersweet feeling. "Shall we meet at the house?"

"I can be there in an hour."

"I'll be waiting."

After they'd hung up, Clem stared at the phone. She wanted to feel encouraged. She wanted to feel hopeful. After all, he had called her. Maybe...

She swallowed. Down deep, she knew nothing had changed. Not really.

And as much as she wanted to believe they could, she was desperately afraid that was just wishful thinking.

Chapter Thirteen

"Will you give me some time?" Luke said.

"Luke..." She had to tell him about the call from Jake Webster. Why hadn't she told him immediately? Why had she put it off? Who was being the coward now?

"I promise you, Clem, I'll find a way to make things work for us." He nuzzled her forehead.

The two of them were sitting close together on the couch. When Clem had first arrived, they'd kissed eagerly, apologizing again for the hurtful things they'd said to each other. Then, in a natural progression, they'd made love. Afterward, Luke fixed dinner for them, and Clem ineptly but gamely helped.

Now it was nearly ten o'clock, and they were sitting with after-dinner drinks and discussing their situation.

But Clem had still not mentioned the call from Jake Webster.

Maybe nothing will come of this. Maybe Webster won't like you when he meets you in person.

Clem sighed.

"What's wrong, Clem?" Luke asked softly. "Are you still upset about last night?"

She pulled back a little and raised her eyes to his. Her heart beat a little faster. "No. It's just that something happened this afternoon. Something I need to tell you about."

"Oh?"

She felt the almost imperceptible stiffening of his body. "I, uh, got a call from Jake Webster at WNN in Chicago." She watched his eyes and knew the instant the meaning behind her words registered.

"What did he have to say?"

Luke's answer was calm, but Clem knew his calm exterior masked the same inner turmoil she felt. "He wants me to come to Chicago on Thursday to talk to him about a job with WNN."

"Wow."

"Yes. Wow."

"This is it, huh? Your big break."

She nodded. Her chest hurt. "Yes. I think so." His eyes had always reminded her of cool green forests spiked with shafts of sunlight. But at this moment the sunlight had disappeared and the forest had been plunged into darkness.

He smiled, and it was a game effort, but she could see his heart wasn't in it. "This is great, Clem. Congratulations."

"Thanks." *Oh, Luke, please say something else. Please tell me how you feel. Let's talk about this....*

"So when are you going? Thursday, did you say?"

"Uh-huh. I'm leaving about one o'clock."

"And when will you be back?"

They could have been talking about the weather, their voices were so dispassionate. "Friday late. Webster said to plan to spend the day on Friday. I guess I'll get the big tour and there'll be lots of people to meet. Several interviews."

He nodded. "But that's really just a formality, isn't it? The job's pretty much yours if you want it."

"That's what I gathered." She forced herself to laugh. "Of course, there's always the possibility that some big shot will take a violent dislike to me. As hard as that is to believe..."

Dutifully he laughed, too. "That *is* hard to believe." And then, unexpectedly, his voice softened and filled with tenderness. He tilted her chin and looked deep into her eyes. "I mean that, Clem. I can't imagine anyone not liking you. You're the most genuine person I've ever met."

When his lips lowered to hers, Clem wanted to cry. *Don't be nice to me! Oh, God, please don't be nice to me.*

The kiss said everything their words had left unsaid. When it was over, Luke said, "I hope everything works out for you, Clem. Whatever it is you want, I hope you get it. You deserve it."

Jake Webster met Clem's flight to O'Hare personally. Clem liked him immediately. He reminded her of

Bradley Stratton. He had the same kind of friendly eyes and genuine, open face.

During the ride from the airport to WNN's head-quarters in downtown Chicago, he gave her a brief history of the network, most of which Clem already knew. "Like CNN, we're a twenty-four-hour news network," he informed her. "Initially, we were only carried by a dozen markets here in the U.S. Today we're carried by every major cable company and indepen-dent station throughout the world."

Clem nodded. Worldwide News Network had had phenomenal success. Was still having phenomenal success.

"The turning point for us was our coverage of the assassination of Freeman Jeppo and the subsequent uprising and revolution in Takanna."

"Yes. I remember." The cable network's coverage had been astounding. They had had reports and pic-tures a full twenty-four hours before anyone else, and by then all viewers were tuned to their broadcast.

He continued to talk about the network, telling her how many people were employed worldwide, in what cities they maintained separate bureaus, the kinds of numbers they'd amassed in terms of regular viewers and some of their expansion plans for the future.

In no time at all they reached their destination.

"I'm going to turn you over to my assistant, Amanda Thorne," Webster said when they got to his office on the twenty-fifth floor. "She'll give you the grand tour, then bring you back here."

"Great," Clem replied.

Amanda Thorne turned out to be a smartly dressed woman of about Clem's age. She smiled warmly and shook Clem's hand. "Nice to meet you."

The next hour was a bewildering array of impressions. Clem was taken to floor after floor, introduced to dozens of people, shown countless offices and film labs and broadcast sets and studios. "Wow," she said more than once.

Amanda smiled. "I know. It's pretty overwhelming the first time you see it."

Later, after Clem had been deposited in Webster's office again, the news director told her about the job. "All of our reporters start as general assignment reporters covering domestic news," he explained. "The first six months to a year are considered the training period. After that, some specialization occurs. About a third of our newer hires stay with general assignment domestic news, about a third go to a new stage of training in covering foreign news and the other third are sent to specialty areas—the Middle East, the Pacific Rim, the African nations, or the Far East." He smiled. "The assignments are based on aptitude and interest."

"It sounds wonderful," Clem said. Finally, she thought. Finally she would get to cover important stories. Finally her dreams were going to come true. She wanted to pinch herself. Maybe she was dreaming.

That night Clem went to dinner with Webster and his wife, a tall brunette who turned out to be a special investigator for the IRS, and Amanda Thorne and her husband, a slightly scruffy-looking man with wild red hair who was a high school chemistry teacher.

After dinner Webster and his wife dropped her at her hotel. "Amanda will be here to pick you up at eight tomorrow morning," Webster told her.

Friday was another whirlwind of activity. Clem was interviewed by several people and had a fairly long session with the head of the Human Resources Department, where she was told about all the benefits and policies of the company.

Then, an hour before she was supposed to leave for the airport and her return trip to Houston, she found herself in Jake Webster's office again. "Well?" he said. "Are you still interested?"

"More than ever." The only hesitation Clem felt had to do with Luke, but somehow, she vowed, she would make things work out for them. She couldn't lose this chance with WNN and she couldn't lose Luke.

"Good. The job is yours, if you want it."

"I want it."

"Can you be ready to move by August fifteenth?"

August 15! That would give her just under three weeks. "Yes."

They shook hands to seal the deal.

Hours later, as her plane jetted its way to the thirty-five-thousand-foot level, Clem repeated her vow.

Somehow, some way, she would make things work out for her and Luke.

It was after nine when Clem reached her apartment. She had promised to call Luke as soon as she got in, and she knew he'd be waiting.

Yet she put off making the call.

She unpacked her suitcase and she fixed herself a diet drink. She kept looking at the phone, but she didn't pick it up.

If only she knew what to do.

If only she knew what Luke's reaction was going to be.

If only she was sure things *would* work out.

She had been so sure, when she told Jake Webster she wanted the job, that she could figure out a way to have it all. But what if she couldn't?

What if, when she told Luke she'd taken the job and how soon she was leaving Houston, he simply said good luck and goodbye? What then?

When Clem still hadn't called him by ten o'clock, Luke called the airline to check on her flight.

"Flight 1135 came in on time, sir," he was told.

He eyed the phone. Surely Clem was home by now. Her flight had landed a few minutes after eight. How long could it take to pick up her bag and retrieve her car and drive home? She should have been home by nine or thereabouts.

He picked up the receiver. A moment later he replaced it. No, he wasn't going to call her. She had said she'd call him, and she would. He walked to the bar and poured himself a couple of fingers of brandy, then carried his glass and the portable phone out to the patio.

The air still carried traces of the heat of the day, but there was a breeze, and the sounds of water cascading over the fountain and the gentle music of the brass wind chimes were more pleasant than the hum of the air conditioner inside, so Luke sat on one of the wrought-iron chairs and sipped at his brandy.

Had Clem been offered the job? he wondered.

Because he loved her, and because he knew it was what she wanted, he hoped it had worked out for her.

But if it had, where did that leave him?

It leaves you here in Houston and her winging her way to Chicago.

Could they maintain a long-distance relationship? Would their feelings for each other survive weeks of absence? Months of absence?

Did Luke even *want* that? How would he feel when she was traipsing all over the place, doing all kinds of exciting things, and he was stuck here in Houston, doing something he had no desire to do? Would he be able to overcome the feelings of resentment and envy that were bound to develop? Wouldn't the prolonged absences and differences in life-style eventually erode their relationship?

Wouldn't she start to feel guilty?

Or worse...what if she felt sorry for him, and continued to see him out of pity?

Might it not be best to set Clem free?

He set his glass down and stared into the night.

At ten-fifteen Clem decided she was being a big coward. A big, big coward. More of a coward than she'd ever been in her life. She and Luke loved each other. They'd find a way to work this out. There was no reason to be afraid.

She picked up the phone.

Luke answered before the first ring was completed.

"I'm coming over," she announced.

"Hurry," he said.

Once again they made love first. But this time there was a desperate quality to the lovemaking, as if each was afraid it might be the last time, even though Clem knew that was silly.

Of course it wouldn't be the last time.

They weren't going to break up, for heaven's sake!

Afterward, he said ruefully, "I think we're both cowards, Clem."

She didn't pretend to misunderstand. Instead, she just held him tighter, pressing her lips against his bare chest. She could feel his heart beating. She closed her eyes.

"You got the job, didn't you?" he asked, stroking her hair.

"Yes."

"When are you going?"

"In three weeks."

"Will you be based in Chicago?"

"Initially, yes." She explained what Jake Webster had said. How in six months or a year she might be assigned to foreign news or sent to a bureau somewhere other than Chicago. "I'll be traveling all the time, though, even from the beginning. I'll go wherever there's a story to be covered."

For a while they were silent as he digested the information and Clem, trying not to think at all, waited. She knew what she wanted to hear him say. But she was desperately afraid he wouldn't say it. *Tell me you'll find a way to get out from under the company. Tell me you'll come with me. Tell me I'm more important than anything else in your life.*

"I'm glad for you," he finally said.

No, no, that isn't what I want to hear.

"This is what you've always wanted."

"Luke—"

"A terrific opportunity," he continued, as if she hadn't spoken. "You're going to love it, and you'll do a spectacular job."

She bit her bottom lip.

He kissed her temple. "I'm going to miss you."

Clem swallowed and tried to still the trembling that began deep inside. She wanted to say, *Why don't you come with me?* but how could she?

What if he didn't want to?

What if, even if he *could* find a way to leave the company, he *still* didn't want to come with her?

"But you're doing the right thing for you," he went on, "and I'm just being selfish wanting you to stay here with me. Besides, we'll still see each other. I can fly up to Chicago some weekends, or wherever you might be, and you can come to Houston when you have time off."

"Sure," Clem echoed. Her heart felt like a stone. "It'll work. We'll still see each other."

"And who knows? Maybe in a year or so I'll be free, too, and then we can see...."

"That would be great."

"And they do say absence makes the heart grow fonder," he said, his voice light. He turned her head so that he could look into her eyes. He was smiling tenderly.

Clem willed herself not to cry. She would not cry. She wouldn't.

"Don't be sad, Clem," he whispered. He kissed her softly. "We've had something great, and it's just like we said in the beginning—no regrets...."

"No. No regrets."

He kissed her again, but no amount of kisses, no amount of touches, no amount of loving could take away the sadness and the bone-deep knowledge that it was over.

Clem had gambled.

And she had lost.

Clem cried all the way home the following morning. She had wanted to go home last night, but she knew she couldn't. So she had spent the night. She'd pretended that everything was fine. That she and Luke hadn't actually said goodbye to each other, even though she knew, and she knew he knew, that they really had.

Oh, they'd see each other again, she knew that, too.

But nothing would ever be the same.

Clem was leaving, moving on.

And Luke was staying put.

Luke spent the most miserable weekend of his life. And Monday morning he called in sick.

He could hear the shocked gasp of surprise from his secretary. "Why," she sputtered, "I can't ever remember you being sick. What's wrong?"

"I think I'm getting the flu," he mumbled. How could he tell her the truth? That he was sick at heart?

He worked furiously around the house all day. He cleaned cabinets and he caulked the bathtub and he fixed a leaky faucet and he weeded flower beds and he cleaned the air-conditioning filter and he changed the oil in his car and he sorted out some clothes to give away and he took other clothing to the dry cleaner and he baked bread—pounding and kneading the dough to the point where he wasn't sure the bread would be any good at all.

But nothing did any good.

About four o'clock he seriously thought about showering and getting dressed up and marching over to Clem's office at the station and carrying her off, caveman style, telling her there was no way he was going to let her leave him. "You're not taking that job, and that's that!" he would say.

He laughed ruefully. Oh, sure. And she'd say, "My hero," in a little, piping voice. *Not.*

Besides, even if Clem would consider turning down the job, did he really want that? She would eventually resent him. The loss of this opportunity would always niggle at the back of her mind, and one day she'd be bound to lash out at him. Eventually their relationship would be ruined because of it.

No, asking Clem not to take the job was not an option.

Unfortunately, there didn't seem to be any other option that Luke liked, either.

"But what about you and Luke?" Annie said.

Clem sighed. "What about us?"

"You love each other, don't you?"

"Yes."

"Well, then . . . what are you going to do?" Annie's voice carried a tinge of exasperation.

Clem sighed again. She could just picture Annie at the other end of the telephone wire—the puzzled look in her eyes and the honest bewilderment she would be feeling. "Annie, what *can* we do? I can't give up this opportunity, and Luke won't leave Houston." *Luke didn't ask me to give up the job.*

"You know, Clem, sometimes I think, for such a smart cookie, you're really very stupid."

"Gee, thanks." *But Annie, he didn't* ask *me not to go!*

"I mean it."

"I know you mean it."

"I'm very disappointed in you."

Clem didn't answer. What was there to say?

Finally Annie must have realized Clem wasn't going to say anything, so she asked, "When are you leaving?"

Clem told her the details.

"Maybe something will work out," Annie offered when Clem was finished.

"Maybe." But Clem didn't think so. And if Annie had seen Luke's face when Clem had left him this morning, she probably wouldn't think so, either.

"I want to have a going-away party for you," Annie said.

"You don't have to do that."

"I know, but I want to."

"Okay." Clem really didn't care one way or the other. The only thing she cared about was Luke.

"Clem . . ." Annie's voice was soft.

"Yeah?"

"I really am happy for you. I know you've worked really hard for this."

"Thanks."

After they hung up, Clem felt more discouraged and unhappy than ever. Even telling Raymond the news and seeing his shocked face didn't give her the rush she'd expected to feel.

She wondered if anything ever would again.

The Saturday of the party dawned hot and overcast. The weathermen predicted rain, perhaps heavy rain. There was a tropical storm hovering on the coastline, and it could move in toward Houston at any moment.

Just what I need, Clem thought glumly.

The past three weeks had been tough. She had worked very hard at her job. She didn't want anyone accusing her of having a lame-duck attitude.

And she had pretty much disposed of all of her belongings that weren't portable or necessary in her new life. The previous day she'd packed up the stuff she couldn't carry in her Jeep and taken it to UPS for shipping.

She had not seen much of Luke. Oh, he'd called, and she'd called, and they'd even gone out to dinner twice, and they'd spent several nights together.

But it wasn't the same.

Their lovemaking was no longer fun. It was permeated with an underlying sadness that refused to go away. And because that was so, they'd become remote from each other.

Clem knew what was happening. Each of them was walling off the part of themselves that hurt and didn't want to hurt more.

Well, soon she wouldn't have to worry about that, because soon she would be gone.

Tonight was the going-away party.

Tomorrow she would leave for Chicago. She and Luke had said their final goodbye last night. He had been invited to the going-away party but told her he didn't think he'd go. "Easier that way," he'd said, and she'd agreed. "Besides, we'll see each other again soon." He'd smiled, but there was a darkness in his eyes.

"Of course we will," she'd replied. *Of course we won't,* she'd thought.

This time, when she'd driven away, she'd been dry-eyed. What was the use in crying?

As Clem got ready for the party and listlessly tried to decide what to wear, she couldn't help remembering the other parties she'd attended in the past few months.

The couples shower and the black slip dress she'd so carefully chosen. Tears formed in her eyes as she remembered the look on Luke's face when he'd spotted her. That was the first night he'd kissed her, too.

And then there was the rehearsal dinner and her royal blue dress. That was the night they first made love.

Clem closed her eyes, remembering the excitement and the delicious newness of it all.

Oh, Luke, Luke, where did we go wrong?

Clem opened her eyes. Actually, she knew exactly where she'd gone wrong. She should have stuck to her original plan. No L words. She should not have fallen in love with him. Falling in love had been her undoing.

Yeah, she thought wryly. Falling in love was definitely not what it was cracked up to be. It certainly hadn't made *her* happier.

Sighing heavily, she decided it didn't really matter what she wore tonight, so she might as well be comfortable. She ended up with a silky red pants outfit that she'd bought several years ago. It was loose and cool and she wouldn't need to wear panty hose, so it was perfect for this kind of weather.

At five o'clock she climbed into her Jeep and took off for the Stratton Ranch.

She wondered if Luke would show up.

She hoped he didn't. She simply couldn't take another goodbye.

Luke decided he wasn't going to the party.

He had no desire to pretend to a happiness he didn't feel or to be surrounded by people who would probably be speculating about him and Clem. Watching them to see how they acted toward each other.

No way.

He would work until midnight. God knows he had enough to do to keep him busy.

Decision made, he resolutely refused to look at the clock and buried his head in the second quarter financial reports.

* * *

Clem pretended to be having fun. She laughed at everyone's jokes and answered questions about her new job and received everyone's congratulations. She ate some of Bradley's famous chili and drank a little beer—not too much, since she had to drive back to Houston, even though Frank and his wife said they'd follow her to make sure she got home all right.

Unknown to Clem, the party had been planned as a "shower." Her family and friends showered her with gifts—some useful, like the Swiss army knife her brother Frank gave her, some frivolous, like the bottle of Joy Annie gave her, and some silly, like the star-shaped sunglasses her sister Valerie gave her. "Because you're going to be a star," Valerie said, grinning.

Clem was touched by her friends' and family's thoughtfulness, but all the while she was poignantly aware that this was the only kind of shower she would ever have.

And all the while, through the eating and talking and opening of gifts, she kept one eye on the clock.

The minute hand crept around.

Nine. Nine-thirty. Ten.

"Gee, I thought for sure Luke would come," Annie said about ten-thirty when she and Clem found themselves alone for a moment.

"I knew he wouldn't," Clem answered. "We said our goodbyes last night."

But she hadn't known. Not really.

And until this moment, when she'd finally accepted that he wasn't coming, she hadn't realized she'd harbored one last secret hope that somehow, some way, he would have managed to work things out. That he'd show up at the party and say, "I'm coming with you tomorrow, Clem."

Oh, you fool.

About eleven the party began to break up. Clem walked around the room and hugged and kissed her parents and sisters and brothers and all their spouses and children. She hugged and kissed her friends next, leaving Annie and Bradley for last.

Annie hugged her tight. "I'll miss you so much," she whispered, tears thickening her voice.

"I'll be home often," Clem promised.

"It won't be the same."

No, it wouldn't be the same. It would never be the same.

And they both knew it.

A little after eleven Clem, accompanied by all the guests, walked outside.

"Goodbye, goodbye," they chorused.

Clem blinked back her tears. Several of the men carried her gifts to her Jeep.

And then she climbed in, waved one last time and pointed her Jeep toward Houston.

Chapter Fourteen

Clem loaded her Jeep and started the long drive to Chicago in a thunderstorm. She couldn't help a wry smile. The weather was a perfect match for her mood, she thought—gray and dark and gloomy.

She had to force herself not to drive past Luke's house on her way out of town. As it was, she blinked back tears when she saw the Houston city limits sign receding in the background.

She had always imagined this day, and in her imagination she'd always been singing at the top of her lungs—thrilled to be leaving Houston behind and exhilarated by the thought of the future.

How different her fantasy was from reality. Today the only emotion she felt was an overwhelming sadness, and as she drove north on U.S. 59 she fought against it. But no matter how hard she tried, she couldn't seem to shake the feeling.

Finally she decided that, okay, today she would indulge herself and wallow in her feelings of grief and loss. But that was it.

After today she would not allow herself to be sad anymore, because there was no percentage in it.

Feeling sad wouldn't change a thing. It certainly wouldn't make Luke love her enough to try to change his life. So tomorrow she would shape up and start focusing on her exciting new job and all the great things life had in store for her.

And who knew? Maybe tomorrow the sun would shine and everything would look different.

Luke didn't go to work on Sunday, even though he'd intended to. Instead he sat in his gloomy house and listened to Beethoven's Fifth Symphony while the thunder and lightning and rain crashed and streaked and pounded around him.

Clem was gone.

The knowledge reverberated inside him just the way the music reverberated in the house and the storm reverberated outside.

He wondered what time she'd left. He'd half hoped, half dreaded the possibility that she'd call him.

She hadn't.

He pictured her loading her Jeep in the rain, probably cussing a little bit as she did it. He smiled. Clem hated when things didn't go her way.

He pictured her giving a jaunty salute as she drove through the gates of her apartment complex.

He pictured her driving west on San Felipe and entering the Loop. Or maybe she hadn't bothered with the Loop. Maybe she'd driven over Weslayan straight to 59.

He knew she planned to take U.S. 59 north to Texarkana, and then Interstate 30 east to Little Rock and then 40 east to Memphis, where she'd pick up Interstate 55 north. They had discussed possible routes for her trip in detail last week, probably because by discussing routes they could avoid discussing what was really on their minds—the dilemma that had no answer.

He pictured her driving in the rain. He hoped she was careful. That Jeep didn't afford much protection from the elements or from other vehicles on the road.

He smiled again.

That Jeep. It suited her. Just the way her clothes suited her and her hairstyle suited her and her skin suited her. That was one of the things he admired most about Clem: the fact that she knew who she was and what she wanted and where she was going and everything she did and wore and said reflected this confidence.

Clem, Clem...how am I going to survive without you now that I know what it's like to have you in my life?

He wondered how long it would take before every waking moment wasn't filled with memories and thoughts of her. A week? A month? A year? A lifetime?

About three o'clock the rain stopped. The sun poked out from the clouds and crept into the house. Luke stirred, and when he did, his stomach rumbled. He finally roused himself from his lethargy and headed for the kitchen.

On the way, he passed the picture of Clem jumping up and down at the softball game that first day—the day they'd met. He stopped. Studied the photograph. It was a wonderful likeness, capturing the essence of Clem—filled with life and energy and passion.

With his forefinger he reached out to touch the image, tracing the lines of her face, her mouth, her outstretched arm.

He would never forget her. No matter how many years went by. No matter what happened to him in the future. No matter who else he might meet, no matter what else he might do. Clem would always be a part of him.

He stood there a long, long time.

Monday morning Clem was feeling better. The sun was shining, and after spending the night in Jackson, Tennessee and having a big breakfast, she was on her way again.

Last night, as she'd lain in the unfamiliar bed and listened to the sounds of the big trucks rumbling by on the interstate, she'd felt more optimistic, and those feelings were reflected in her more upbeat attitude today.

It simply wasn't in Clem's nature to be unhappy or pessimistic for long. And who knew? Maybe when she got to Chicago she'd call Luke and find out he'd had a change of heart. After all, miracles *did* happen once in a while.

Monday morning at nine o'clock Luke called a meeting. He had telephoned his mother the night before, so she was there along with his brothers, his sister and Alex Costas, who now owned a share of the company.

"I want out," Luke announced when they were all seated around the conference table. "I no longer want to run the company."

Everyone stared at him. "Wh-what do you mean?" Paul asked, obviously stunned.

"Just what I said. I never wanted to do this kind of work for a living. You all know the story. I wanted to be a photographer. That's what I was studying in school. Well, I really didn't have much of a choice when Dad died. I had to step in and learn this business. The rest of you were too young, and Mom couldn't have done it. But that was sixteen years ago." He looked around at his mother, his siblings. "Everyone here is grown-up now. It's time for me to get out and do the things I want to do before it's too late."

His mother slowly nodded. "I was wondering when you'd come to this conclusion," she said.

"I had no idea you felt this way," Mark murmured.

"Me, either," added John.

Alex Costas didn't say anything, and Luke wondered what the older man was thinking.

"I've tried to tell all of you how I feel. I approached each one of you," he declared, looking at his brothers one by one, "about taking over my job."

"But we didn't think you *meant* it," Paul protested. He looked at the others.

"No," Matthew echoed, "we thought you were just griping. You know. Like we all do once in a while."

"No," Luke said, "I wasn't just griping."

"So what do you propose we do, Luke?" Alex finally asked. "Do you have any suggestions?"

"Well, ideally, one of you could take over as president," Luke said. "But if none of you want to, or no one feels capable of doing the job, I suppose we could hire someone." He paused. "Or... we could sell the company. You all know that Fleming has shown an interest in the past." Fleming Security was the largest security company in the nation and had made a practice of buying out smaller companies.

"Sell the business!" Mark exclaimed. "We can't—"

"If we don't sell the business," his mother interrupted, "what about your share, Luke? Did you mean for one of us to buy you out?"

Luke shrugged. "If one of you wanted to buy me out, I'd be happy to sell, but I don't need to." He smiled. "I'll be just as happy to share in the profits at the end of the year, like any ordinary shareholder."

She nodded.

"I'm not in favor of selling the company," Alex said. "I just bought a piece of it—" he smiled at Rebecca "—thanks to your sister, and I like being a part owner."

"No, I don't want to sell, either," agreed John.

The others slowly echoed the same sentiments, although Mark said wistfully, "I don't know. It's kind of appealing to think of having a chunk of money to do something with. Miranda and I would kind of like to go into the bed-and-breakfast business someday and—"

"Forget it, Mark!" Paul and Matthew chorused.

"Oh, okay," Mark grumbled good-naturedly. "I was only kidding. But what are we going to do? Who's going to take over Luke's responsibilities? Are we going to hire someone?"

"I don't know if I'm in favor of hiring someone," John said. "Maybe between the five of us—us four brothers and Alex—we could split the responsibilities."

The others chimed in, and before Luke knew it, a lively discussion was in progress about who could do what.

Luke stood. "Well, since I'm no longer going to be a working part of the company, I'll let the rest of you decide how you're going to handle my leaving. Because right now I've got a plane to catch."

"Where are you going, Luke?" Rebecca asked.

"To Chicago."

His mother smiled. "Give her my love."

* * *

By Monday afternoon Clem's optimism had faded and she was once more mired in gloom.

Who was she kidding?

She and Luke were finished.

Kaput.

Her thoughts continued in this vein for the rest of her trip. She even began to wonder if she was doing the right thing. Was a job more important than the man she loved?

But he didn't ask you to give up the job. . . .

She sighed heavily.

He didn't love you enough.

"Shut up!" she shouted to the air. "I don't want to think about it!"

Luke was lucky.

He was able to get on a one-o'clock flight to Chicago, which would put him in the city in the late afternoon. Since he knew Clem would arrive no sooner than seven or eight that night, he should beat her by several hours.

He grinned.

What would she do when she saw him there?

It took Clem longer than she thought it would to get to Chicago. By the time she reached the city, found her exit and drove to her hotel, it was nearly ten o'clock. She was glad she'd guaranteed her arrival.

"Yes, Miss Bennelli," the front desk clerk said, "we've been expecting you." He gave her a funny look.

Clem wondered what his problem was. Did she have a pimple on her nose, or something? He kept casting surreptitious glances at her as he checked her in. And it seemed to her that he was trying not to smile. She decided he was amused by her appearance. She guessed she *did* look pretty ratty in her faded army green shorts with all the pockets, her favorite hiking boots and her T-shirt that proclaimed If A Woman Were Running The World, It Would Never Need An Overhaul.

She waited impatiently as the clerk took her credit card to make an impression, explained about the coded room key, then handed it over.

"That's 1155," he said. "Remember, it's not marked on the key. That way, if you lose it, no one knows what room it opens."

Clem almost told him she wasn't that much of a hick that she didn't know about unmarked keys, but she decided it would be a waste of breath.

"Enjoy your stay with us, Miss Bennelli."

"Thanks."

The bellman said he'd meet her at her room, so Clem picked up her small overnight bag and headed for the bank of elevators. When she reached the eleventh floor she headed down the wrong wing and had to double back before she found her room.

She set her overnight bag on the floor and inserted her key into the lock. The lock flashed red.

"Darn it. I hate these darned cards."

She inserted the card again. This time it flashed green and she hurriedly turned the door handle before the lock changed its mind and flashed red again.

The door swung open. She bent to pick up her bag, then straightened and walked into her room.

And nearly fainted.

The room was filled with dozens of bouquets of daisies. And standing in the middle of them, at the foot of the king-size bed that dominated the room, just as big as life and grinning like a fool, was Luke. In his hands was a daisy. He was pulling off the petals one by one. "She loves me, she loves me not. She—"

"Loves you!" Clem shouted, catapulting herself into his arms.

"What took you so long?" he asked as they tumbled backward onto the bed.

"Luke, oh, Luke," she said, planting kisses all over his face.

He laughed. "Oh, Clem, it's so good to see you."

They kissed and kissed and kissed.

Finally he let her up for air. "What are you *doing* here?" she asked.

Before he could answer, there was a sharp knock at the door.

"That's gotta be the bellman with my bags."

"Let me up, and I'll go let him in," Luke said.

As Luke walked to the door and opened it, Clem smoothed back her hair and tried to look as if she hadn't been lying on the bed getting thoroughly kissed.

The bellman's eyebrows went up when he saw the daisies. Clem smothered a smile.

Luke tipped him, and the bellman left.

"Now tell me everything!" she demanded.

They sat on the edge of the bed, and he explained everything that had happened since yesterday. How he'd thought about all the things she'd said to him.

"You were right, you know. I guess I never really wanted anything badly enough to just go for it. But last night, looking at your picture, I realized I did want something badly enough now. I wanted you." He put his arm around her and hugged her close. "God, I love you, Clem."

"I love you, too."

He smiled down at her. "I also wanted to try to make a go of my photography. So I made a decision." He told her about the meeting he'd had that morning.

"You mean you've left the company? For good?"

"Yes."

"Oh, my God!" Clem was so happy she was afraid she'd burst. "I can't believe it. I just can't believe it!"

"Of course, I'll have to go back to Houston. I've got a house to sell and some other things to take care of, but then I plan to join you here in Chicago and start working on my own career."

"Why are you selling your house? I love your house."

"Well, frankly, Clem, I'm going to need the money. After all, it might take me years to earn enough from my photography to live on."

"It doesn't matter. I make enough to support us both."

"There's no way I'm going to let you support me," he said stubbornly. "No way."

"Why not? If the shoe was on the other foot, I'm sure you'd be willing to support me."

"That's different."

"How is it different?"

He laughed. "I'm not going to win this argument, am I?"

"No, you're not."

"Okay, okay, I give up. I won't sell my house right away. I'll just cash in some of my stocks and see how things go. But I'm paying my fair share of our expenses."

She smiled. "It's a deal. I'm so glad you're going to keep the house. It'll be nice knowing it's there, don't you think? A place to come home to between assignments. You *are* planning to travel with me, aren't you?"

"Try to keep me away." He reached for her again.

After a long kiss that made Clem's heart race and her body clamor for more, she said breathlessly, "Does this mean you want to get married?"

He grinned. "Heck, no. I think it'll be more fun to live in sin, don't you?"

"Oh, absolutely." But Clem crossed her fingers behind her back. She had no intention of ever letting Luke get away.

"Now shut up and kiss me, woman," he demanded with a mock growl.

"Your wish is my command."

As Clem's arms closed around Luke she suddenly thought of her mother and her sisters and Annie and how happy all of them would be, and she smiled.

"What?" Luke whispered.

"Oh, nothing," she replied. "I was just thinking how happy I am. I don't think I could be any happier than I am right this minute."

"Oh, yeah? Wanna bet?" he teased. "I'll bet I can make you a *lot* happier." As he talked, his hand crept under her T-shirt.

And you know what?

He was right.

Epilogue

"You know, Luke, I sure am glad you finally decided to make an honest woman of me."

Luke lowered the new camera he'd purchased with the sale of his first photo spread to *Newstime* magazine. "*I* finally decided?" He gave Clem an amused look. She was sitting Indian fashion on the bed in the London hotel room which had been their domicile the past two days while she covered the British elections. "I decided?" he repeated. "Don't you think you're twisting the facts just a little bit?"

"Who, me?" She gave him one of her most innocent expressions, but she couldn't maintain it for long. "Okay, *we* decided."

"No, my love," Luke contradicted gently, walking over to sit beside her and drawing her into his arms.

"*You* decided. I wanted to marry you all along. But it took *you* eighteen months to realize that's what you wanted, too."

She started to protest, but he silenced her by kissing her. One kiss led to another. And another. The desire and need that had only increased as his love for her deepened flared quickly into life. He began to unbutton her blouse.

"Wait, wait," she said breathlessly. "I have something to tell you."

"It better be important," Luke grumbled, pretending to be annoyed. "'Cause I want you, woman, and you know how I hate to be kept waiting."

"Is sex all you ever think about?" she said, pretending right along with him.

"What else is there?" he teased.

"Well . . . in about seven months, there's going to be a lot else. . . ."

It took Luke a few minutes to snap to her meaning. He stared at her, stunned. "You're pregnant?"

She grinned, eyes shining. "Yes! I went to the doctor last week. He says I'm seven weeks along." Her grin got wider and she gave Luke a mock punch. "That's fast work, buster, considering we've only been married for ten weeks."

The wildest joy filled Luke, rendering him speechless.

"Well?" Clem said. "Say something. You're happy, aren't you?"

"Happy!" he exclaimed, finally finding his voice. "I'm ecstatic. I can hardly believe it. I'm gonna be a father!"

She laughed with delight. "And I haven't even told you the best part!"

"The best part?"

Her expression became mischievous. "Must you repeat *everything* I say?"

"Clem . . ." he warned.

The mischief faded as her gaze met his. "The doctor says I'm carrying twins."

Luke hadn't believed that he could be any happier, but her announcement sent his heart skyrocketing. "Are you serious?"

She nodded.

"Oh, Clem." He swallowed against the sudden lump in his throat.

Her smile was tremulous.

Gently, he enfolded her into his arms, holding her close and kissing the top of her head. "I'm the luckiest man on earth."

"And I'm the luckiest woman." She raised her face to look at him. "I love you so much," she whispered.

"I love you more."

"No, I love you more."

He laughed softly. "If you love me so much, why don't you stop talking and show me?"

And so she did.

* * * * *

#1027 PART-TIME WIFE—Susan Mallery
That Special Woman!/Hometown Heartbreakers

When Jill Bradford took the position of nanny to three adorable boys, she was determined that it stay a business arrangement. But the boys' father, Craig Haynes, wanted more than just a part-time mother or wife. He wanted Jill forever.

#1028 EXPECTANT FATHER—Leanne Banks

Caleb Masters was intelligent, gorgeous—everything Glory Danson desired in a man. Becoming pregnant with his child, she married for the sake of the baby…but would the expectant father and mom-to-be find love ever after?

#1029 ON MOTHER'S DAY—Andrea Edwards
Great Expectations

When Alex Rinehart reunited Fiona Scott with the daughter she'd given up for adoption, he helped her save the child she thought she'd never see again. And now that Alex and Fiona had found each other, Fiona had more than one reason to celebrate on Mother's Day.

#1030 NEW BRIDE IN TOWN—Amy Frazier
Sweet Hope Weddings

Belle Sherman had arrived and the town of Sweet Hope—and its most eligible bachelor, Boone O'Malley—would never be the same again. When these opposites attracted, there was no stopping Belle from being the next bride in town, unless her groom got cold feet!

#1031 RAINSINGER—Ruth Wind

Daniel Lynch was a drop-dead handsome Navajo with black eyes and an attitude to match. And suddenly Winona Snow found herself sharing her house with him! Soon this stubborn man held the key to her future…and her heart.

#1032 MARRY ME, NOW!—Allison Hayes

She had to save the ranch, but first Dacy Fallon needed to convince old flame Nick Reynolds to accept her help. He wouldn't admit that the old attraction was as strong as ever, but Dacy was determined to win herself a cowboy groom.…

MILLION DOLLAR SWEEPSTAKES
AND EXTRA BONUS PRIZE DRAWING

SILHOUETTE... Where Passion Lives

Don't miss these Silhouette favorites by some of our most distinguished authors! And now you can receive a discount by ordering two or more titles!

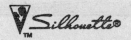

As seen on TV!
Free Gift Offer

With a Free Gift proof-of-purchase from any Silhouette® book,
you can receive a beautiful cubic zirconia pendant.

This gorgeous marquise-shaped stone is a genuine cubic
zirconia—accented by an 18" gold tone necklace.

(Approximate retail value $19.95)

Send for yours today...
compliments of ▼ *Silhouette*®
™

To receive your free gift, a cubic zirconia pendant, send us one original proof-of-
purchase, photocopies not accepted, from the back of any Silhouette Romance™,
Silhouette Desire®, Silhouette Special Edition®, Silhouette Intimate Moments®
or Silhouette Shadows™ title available in February, March or April at your favorite
retail outlet, together with the Free Gift Certificate, plus a check or money order for
$1.75 U.S./$2.25 CAN. (do not send cash) to cover postage and handling, payable
to Silhouette Free Gift Offer. We will send you the specified gift. Allow 6 to 8 weeks for
delivery. Offer good until April 30, 1996 or while quantities last. Offer valid in the U.S. and
Canada only.

Free Gift Certificate

Name: _____

Address: _____

City: _____ State/Province: _____ Zip/Postal Code: _____

Mail this certificate, one proof-of-purchase and a check or money order for postage
and handling to: SILHOUETTE FREE GIFT OFFER 1996. In the U.S.: 3010 Walden
Avenue, P.O. Box 9057, Buffalo NY 14269-9057. In Canada: P.O. Box 622, Fort Erie,

---

FREE GIFT OFFER   079-KBZ-R
ONE PROOF-OF-PURCHASE
To collect your fabulous FREE GIFT, a cubic zirconia pendant, you must include this
original proof-of-purchase for each gift with the properly completed Free Gift Certificate.

079-KBZ-R

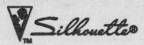